MELVIN R. WEAVER
2213 LEABROOK RD.
LANCASTER, PA 17603
717-569-6576

THE JOSEPH SCROLL

An Exciting Historical Novel

by

Clifford Wilson, Ph.D.

MASTER BOOKS
A Division of CLP
San Diego, California

THE JOSEPH SCROLL

Copyright © 1979
MASTER BOOKS, A Division of CLP
P.O. Box 15666
San Diego, California 92115

Library of Congress Catalog Card Number 78-65633
ISBN 0-89051-054-7

ALL RIGHTS RESERVED

No part of this publication may be reproduced, stored in a retrieval system, or transmitted in any form or by any means—electronic, mechanical, photocopy, recording, or otherwise—without the express prior permission of Master Books, with the exception of brief excerpts in magazine articles and/or reviews.

Cataloging in Publication Data:

Wilson, Clifford Allen, 1923-
  The Joseph Scroll.

1. Joseph of Arimathea—fiction.
I. Title

78-65633

Printed in the United States of America

Cover by Marvin Ross

The Joseph Scroll

by Rabbi Joseph ben Torah
as interpreted by
Clifford Wilson

To avoid misunderstandings and accusations of fraudulence, we immediately make it clear that this is an "interpretation" in the sense that the author has by proxy put himself in the place of Joseph of Arimathea . . . and lived those days with him.

The author's own background as an archaeologist, author, and theologian have been highly relevant in this penetrating analysis.

CONTENTS

		Page
Introduction:	*The Story Must Be Told*	xi
Letter 1:	*I Was Too Late For The Trial of Christ*	1
Letter 2:	*Signs And Wonders: The Works Of Jesus*	9
Letter 3:	*Rabbi Nicodemus Meets Jesus At Night*	21
Letter 4:	*Courage In A Den Of Thieves*	29
Letter 5:	*The King On A Donkey*	39
Letter 6:	*The Plot Against Lazarus*	47
Letter 7:	*The Illegal Trial of Jesus*	51
Letter 8:	*I Walked Behind Jesus*	63
Letter 9:	*The Sun Was Darkened*	77
Letter 10:	*I Begged The Body Of Jesus*	89
Letter 11:	*Jesus Left The Tomb*	101
Letter 12:	*The Resurrection of Jesus The Christ*	121
Letter 13:	*"Don't Fight Against God!"*	131
Letter 14:	*Nicodemus Debates With The Rabbis*	143
Letter 15:	*Saul's Misguided Fury*	151
Letter 16:	*I Must Go Into Hiding . . .*	155

The Author

Clifford Wilson is a widely known educator and archaeologist from Australia and has a Ph.D. from the University of South Carolina. For some years he was Director of the Australian Institute of Archaeology and was an Area Supervisor at the excavation at Gezer, Israel, in 1969. He has gained popularity as author of *Crash Go The Chariots, That Incredible Book the Bible, Approaching the Decade of Shock, Close Encounters: A Better Explanation,* and many other widely-read books.

His background in archaeology makes him eminently qualified to write this fascinating novel about the events surrounding the most exciting period in all history.

To my friend Lazarus . . . . and to all those who shall know newness of life through Him Who laid in my tomb.

INTRODUCTION

I was there . . . at the trial before Pontius Pilate . . . at Golgotha . . . at the tomb when we gently laid the body of Jesus inside.

I was not there . . . at the trial of Jesus by my Jewish colleagues, for by the time I reached Jerusalem He had already been arraigned before Pontius Pilate, the Roman Procurator.

I was there . . . when they nailed Him on to a wooden cross . . . when they jolted it down into that prepared hole . . . when He cried, "Father, forgive them . . . ."

I was there . . . when the sun was darkened . . . when the earth was quaking beneath our feet . . . when the Roman Centurion cried out, "Surely this was the Son of God!"

I was there . . . before Pontius Pilate, to beg the body of Jesus . . . when he was officially told that Jesus was indeed dead . . . and I witnessed his amazement when he was informed.

I was there . . . when we wrapped His body in linen and carried it gently to my own garden tomb . . . when we placed that body inside the tomb . . . when the stone was rolled across the front of my tomb . . . .

Because I was there and witnessed so much, my story must be told. I shall do so in a series of letters which shall then be safely hidden. That is to say, I shall do so provided I live long enough to fulfill my plan, for at present I walk in danger of my life. You shall be able to judge if my work was brought to its conclusion.

Maranatha! The Lord comes!

Letter No. 1

I Was Too Late For The Trial Of Christ

Others have begun to write concerning the events of the last few months, and it is appropriate that I should add my testimony. Because I was a member of the Great Sanhedrin I have access to some matters that are not commonly known, and as I have now publicly identified myself with Jesus called the Christ, it seems to me that I should put on record certain facts which I want to be known to our sons and to their sons after them. My own life is now in danger, and I shall leave this scroll in a safe place with other papers, to be opened only after my death.

It was I who saw to it that Jesus the Christ was given decent burial. My colleagues in the Sanhedrin wanted His body to be thrown onto the city rubbish heap outside our holy City of Jerusalem, but I went to Pontius Pilate, the Procurator, and begged for the body. He gave me the permission I sought, and, with the help of my friend Rabbi Nicodemus, the body of Jesus was laid in my own garden tomb. Some of the women who followed Jesus helped with the spices and ointments. I shall tell you more as we proceed.

The tomb itself was not yet fully constructed, for it had been my intention for it to be the last resting place of my wife and myself. It is of course a double tomb.

I was not personally present during the preliminary trials of Jesus, for the messenger from the High Priest in Jerusalem did not reach my village of Arimathea until the early hours of the morning. I immediately arose and was transported by chariot directly to the High Priest's palace. However, the cocks were crowing as we entered the Damascus Gate. We had covered those 15 Roman miles in a remarkably short time, and by all normal standards of Jewish legal practice we should have been at the scene of the trial long before it even began. <u>A trial dealing with a capital charge should not be held at night time</u>.

A further <u>point is that a "guilty" verdict cannot be ratified until at least a complete</u>

<u>day has passed. That was ignored in this case.</u>

To my great surprise, the trial had not only begun when we arrived at dawn, but it had also been irrevocably concluded. I did my best to gain an interview with either Annas or Caiaphas, but I was quite unsuccessful. My protest was irrelevant, and indeed it was a possible embarrassment. In any case, they were far too involved in ensuring that their plan was carried through to its final conclusion. They were determined to do that before any appeal could be sustained, or the Jerusalem crowd with its many pilgrims be stirred into a counter-offensive, demanding the release of the Prisoner. Many of them believed Him to be the Christ, the Prophet like unto Moses Who should come into the world.

It was the events of that morning that suddenly made me a more open convert to the cause of Jesus the Christ, and my previous reactions and attitudes should be seen in that light. Nicodemus and I were alike in that we believed that Jesus, the Prophet from Galilee, must be the One for Whom we were searching, but we were secret believers. Strangely, it was His death that finally brought us both to the place of open confession. Many things fell into place, and we were drawn together by an overwhelming conviction that this thing was of God. Rabbi Gamaliel was another who almost sided with us, as we shall see, but not quite. He is deeply concerned, and is pondering many things that disturb him. Perhaps in a coming day he will see the truth and act according to his conscience. I am convinced that this will also be true of many of my priestly brethren.

Before they crucified the Christ, I had first given serious thought to the possibility that He was an impostor, a false Christ who was deliberately deceiving the world. To me it was quite unacceptable that a man could claim to be equal with God, for we Jews commonly hold such a claim to be sheer blasphemy. If Jesus made such assertions He would be guilty of either a capital offense or of insanity—that is unless His claim were true.

How could such a claim be substantiated? We believe in God, but we believe also in evil powers. Thus even seeming miracles would not necessarily prove that a man was a representative of God, for he might well be undertaking lying signs and wonders. Some of my colleagues claimed Jesus was in league with Beelzebub, the prince of the demons. For some time I personally was not convinced either way. Both His opponents and His disciples seemed equally convinced and convincing, and to decide where the truth lay was not easy.

I lived at Arimathea, and most of Jesus' great works were undertaken at some distance from my village. True, two of His disciples had preached in our town quite early in His ministry, and there were reports of miraculous healings by those men at that time. However, we do get such reports from time to time, and I had not been especially impressed, or even interested.

I had shrugged my shoulders as it were. Even if healings had taken place, it was possible that someone merely had faith in that particular "healer." Or maybe it was a demonstration of evil powers, and if so, the whole thing should be rejected anyway.

Until the reports became more consistent it was easy to use such terms as "hoax," "fake," and a colloquial term "quack," which we use to apply to a charlatan who has the effrontery to claim healing powers. However, soon the reports were of such a nature that we could no longer hide our heads in the sand. It seemed that the

Sanhedrin should now act.

They should have dispassionately examined the claims of Jesus, and then decided their course of action. However, at no time did they consider the possibility that He really was Who He claimed to be, the Messiah of God. His miracles were never properly investigated, and in retrospect that is incredible, for the evidences were widespread and could have been examined with little trouble.

Nor were His teachings taken seriously. If they had been, it could have been shown that all He said was in conformity with our own Scriptures.

Even the writings of the Essenes made it clear that others of our people recognized the fact that a Messiah was to be expected in our times. In view of all this, it really was strange that the only official deliberation about Jesus was concerning the best way to entangle Him in His talk, or to denounce Him as a servant of Beelzebub the prince of the demons, or to show that He had broken the law about Sabbath-keeping by His healing the sick on the Sabbath.

If they doubted the genuineness of His claims, they should have called as witnesses some of those He healed. One such

I WAS TOO LATE FOR THE TRIAL OF CHRIST

man they called had been born blind, and Jesus healed him. When the leaders saw that his story was apparently true, their <u>reaction was to have him cast out of the synagogue. They were interested only in evidence against Jesus, not for Him</u>. They even came to the point of openly scheming to put him to death.

And of course their paying blood-money to the traitor Judas of Iscaria was a total rejection of our own law which specifically states that a capital offense cannot be brought to a head by such a payment.

The facts are clear. The evidence was never properly considered, and the charges were not even legally formulated. The case against Jesus the Christ was determined before he was ever brought to trial. It was clearly a total miscarriage of justice.

Letter No. 2

Signs And Wonders: The Works of Jesus

I have said that initially it was not easy to decide whether the claims of Jesus were true or false. However, before He was crucified I had become convinced that in truth God was empowering Him. I had come to the point of believing that no ordinary mortal could undertake what He did, by normal means.

Possibly some of the stories of His life will become embellished with time, and skeptics will be inclined to throw out everything because some things will be exaggerated. Already there are false stories about miracles in the boyhood of Jesus. Therefore I want to record the basic facts about some events, while they are still fresh in my mind. In every case they have been told to me by at least two reputable witnesses, including some of the earliest disciples of Jesus. I have been careful to observe the requirements of our own Law, for example in the mouths of two or three witnesses every word should be established. Also, I have carefully selected a variety of incidents which point to different aspects of the deity of Jesus the Christ.

Early in His public appearances there was a report that He turned water into wine. At first we all mocked and quite refused to take the incident seriously. It was at the marriage of a family friend of Jesus, and we considered it to be a family story, loyally supported by credulous relatives and a few simple-minded artisans who found it more congenial to become His companions than to do a good day's work. In any case, after men have drunk for a while, their minds are affected, and a man with good suggestive powers might even make them think water was wine. Or perhaps they were so affected that they would not notice if a large quantity of water was added to the last dregs of the wine.

"Cheap trickery," was the vehement announcement of some of my Sanhedrin colleagues. At that stage the works of Jesus had not reached the ears of the leading priests such as Annas and

SIGNS AND WONDERS: THE WORKS OF JESUS 11

Caiaphas.

On another occasion it was reported that Jesus had miraculously fed 5,000 men, as well as many women and children. The claim was that a little boy gave up his lunch, that Jesus had the crowds sit down on the grass, then He prayed, and gave the food to His friends who in turn handed it out along the rows of people. Before long everybody had enough. Again we were not convinced.

"No doubt they were all shamed into sharing, following the boy's example," was the explanation we settled for. Even when Jesus did it a second time, this time with a slightly smaller crowd, we again grasped at the explanation put forward.

"The crowd is smaller this time. People are beginning to see through his trickery!"

Looking back, Nicodemus and I have both realized the force of a statement by our great prophet, Isaiah, "Having eyes, they see not. Having ears they hear not." Truly, we all have physical eyes and ears, but we Jews spiritually were blind and deaf to the obvious spiritual realities before us. We were all amazingly gullible and credulous when it came to believing the explanations of our priestly colleagues, but unready to believe the obvious truths of

God before our eyes.

Our spiritual blindness was great. We heard of the blind having their sight restored, of the deaf hearing, of the lame walking. We heard of demons being cast out of men who had been demented for years and of a man with a withered hand being healed. Men and women, boys and girls, young and old—the stories were multiplying, but always in those early days we listened to plausible explanations, and we refused to take this "miracle-worker" seriously. As I say, looking back our attitudes were incredible. Perhaps I should add that this was not true of Nicodemus. I know now that he was a secret believer for some time before I was.

Just the same, some of us were having strange doubts about our attitudes, and we were increasingly unconvinced by the arguments now being foisted on us by some of our ruling group, headed by Caiaphas. Even though in the early days we Jewish leaders laughed loudly at people being so gullible as to believe in such nonsensical claims, the laughter became softer, and then it gave way to smiles, and then to neutral silence. Then there came this uneasy feeling, deep down in our beings, that perhaps we were wrong.

Eventually Nicodemus and I shared our growing belief. We found we had both passed beyond the stage of skepticism. We became convinced, but as yet we would not openly announce ourselves as disciples because we were afraid of our leaders. It was not until Jesus was crucified that we were finally courageous enough to come out into the open, no matter what the cost. Now we were totally convinced, and that meant the end of our fear. Then we took our places in the forefront of the priestly believers in Jesus.

A great number of our colleagues have since taken a similar stand. They were not actually following us, but it is true that we were the first of the priestly company to declare ourselves. Would to God we had declared ourselves earlier—and yet, that is only said because of my personal shame at my cowardice. Did not our own prophets point to that? And so God overruled, and in a sense our cowardice was immaterial.

There have been a number of other incidents that Nicodemus and I have discussed over the last three years, incidents that made us begin to realize that Jesus was indeed our Messiah, and the Savior of the world. One was when Jesus healed a little boy, the son of a nobleman whom we both knew. It was not only the healing of the dying boy that impressed us, though that was remarkable enough. The most amazing part, so we agreed, was that Jesus did not go to the man's house, but simply spoke the word from a distance. At that very moment the boy was healed.

We were still not totally convinced, for life is full of strange coincidences. Many people recover from the point of death, and such a happy timing would no doubt help to establish Jesus as the prophet sent from God. Nevertheless, there was a persistent feeling that just possibly Jesus really was Who He claimed to be. If He really could speak the word from a distance and a dying boy was healed, this pointed to three major attributes of deity. It would mean that Jesus was omniscient, having all knowledge: He knew the symptoms, without having to be personally present and to diagnose. It would also point to His omnipotence, having all power, for He could not only diagnose but He could also prescribe and cure, merely by an act of His will.

Third, it would point to the possibility of His not being limited by space as we are, for He did not need to come personally or physically to the location where the boy

SIGNS AND WONDERS: THE WORKS OF JESUS 15

was lying ill.

As I say, we were not completely convinced, Nicodemus and I, but we were no longer agreeing or laughing with our cynical colleagues.

Then came reports of a lame man being healed at the Pool of Bethesda outside Jerusalem, near the Sheep Gate. This case could not be easily refuted, because everybody knew of this particular man. He had lain there year after year, a helpless cripple, having to be carried everywhere. He simply lay there on a mattress, hoping for alms from any who came to visit this beautiful pool, widely known as the Pool with Five Porches.

Our Jewish tradition was that an angel came down each year and stirred the waters. Whoever got in first after that happened was healed. This man could not move very quickly and therefore could never be the first in after the pool-stirring.

Now the reports reached us that Jesus came to the Pool and spoke quietly to the man. Those nearby saw him suddenly stand up, pick up his mattress, and literally walk off.

"Collusion and trickery," our priestly group assured any who were impressed. "The man was never lame. He had a good income as a beggar—why bother to work?"

Although the man had been a well-known figure, we allowed ourselves to be silenced. He was almost an institution to our people, for most of us had known about him all our lives. Now we were expected to believe he had always been a fake. Yet, if that were the case, why had he bothered to walk just when Jesus came along, and so throw away that lucrative begging bowl? It did not make sense.

Not only had Nicodemus and I stopped laughing. By now we had even stopped nodding in agreement and smiling at the plausible explanations put forward by the vociferous opponents of the Man Who was claiming to undertake miraculous activities by the power of God.

We were fast becoming convinced. In fact, Nicodemus *was* convinced, but he feared our leaders. If I had been convinced and had identified with the movement, I'm sure Nicodemus would have joined me, even as he did after the crucifixion when we begged for the body of Jesus. All he needed was the moral support of one colleague. Eventually I was that colleague.

One other episode that I found to be really convincing concerned a blind man. As with the lame man who was brought day after day to the Pool of Bethesda, this man was almost an institution in Jerusalem. He was a beggar, and he had been born blind. One day Jesus met him and told him to go and wash in the Pool of Siloam, and the report was that he did as he was told—he washed in that Pool—and he was able to see. His faith led to his gaining his sight.

At the time when that beggar was given his sight, some of the Jews challenged the man's parents as to whether he was their son, and then as to whether he really had been born blind.

"He is our son," they answered, "And he was indeed born blind. But we do not know how he is now able to see—ask our son himself!"

I know why they spoke like that. My colleagues had resolved that anybody who acknowledged Jesus as the Messiah would be put out of the synagogue. To many of my people such excommunication would be worse than death. That threat effectively silenced many of those who might otherwise had announced themselves in support of Jesus.

However, the formerly blind man was not to be silenced, and he insisted that Jesus had healed him. In a way, this was the point of no return for many. This evidence for the genuineness of what Jesus was doing was, to say the least, hard to refute. To further reject His claims involved a closing of the mind—deliberate spiritual blindness. Many did just that, including some of our priestly group. At that point they had already cast their votes in favor of the crucifixion of Jesus, for they were insisting that He was a false Christ, a blasphemer who undertook the works of Beelzebub while claiming to demonstrate the power of God.

Suddenly I saw some things clearly, for it was forcibly borne in upon me that my priestly colleagues would not accept the claims of Jesus under any circumstances. Spiritually they were as blind as that man who had been physically blind. I knew that some of them were as uneasy as I was, and after that incident a group of them actually asked Jesus if, in His opinion, they also were blind. He told them quite openly that they were willfully guilty of what amounted to spiritual blindness.

Others of our Pharisee party took another stand at that time. The man who had received his sight had been brought before us, and we listened to his claims. Some of my colleagues said the claims could not be

SIGNS AND WONDERS: THE WORKS OF JESUS 19

true, for there were reports that some of the other healings of Jesus had been undertaken on the Sabbath day, even as this one had been. However, there were the beginnings of a hardening against the "official" line. For the first time, some of us stood up openly to the "Christ-opponents." Previously we had talked together only in ones and twos, as with Nicodemus and myself, but now we said clearly, "If he is a sinner as you claim, how can he undertake an amazing miracle such as this one?"

They were not convinced of course, but from that time on the division was clearcut. Some of us believe we were not there in time for the midnight trial of Christ because of the opinions we expressed that day. We were becoming an embarrassment to the "official" party.

Letter No. 3

Rabbi Nicodemus Meets Jesus At Night

I want to tell you about an incident associated with my friend Rabbi Nicodemus. He asked for a personal interview with Jesus at nighttime, to avoid the crush of the crowds around Him in the daylight hours. Even Annas and Caiaphas have a high regard for Nicodemus, and among our colleagues of the Great Sanhedrin he is referred to as "The Teacher."

Let me say in passing that Nicodemus also was not present at the trial of Jesus. Like myself, he was informed in the middle of the night of the intended trial, and he was amazed to find that he was too late to cast his vote. I shall elaborate on that as we proceed. I am convinced that Annas

and Caiaphas would not have wanted
Nicodemus present at that trial, for his
legal knowledge would have embarrassed
them. Nicodemus would have insisted on
proper procedures being followed. In his
absence it was much easier to proceed
ruthlessly, without pretense of following the
judicial practices which our Law demands.

Nicodemus had gone to Jesus at nighttime, three years before that final trial.
Like myself, he had been very impressed
with the miracles about which everyone
was talking throughout all Judea.

"No one can do the things you are doing
unless God is with him," Nicodemus said
to Jesus. Jesus gave an answer that surprised Nicodemus.

"You must be born again."

Nicodemus had expected to discuss the
miracles, and to consider the evidence
pointing to Jesus as the Messiah. Instead,
he listened to a new teaching about a
rebirth.

Jesus said something else that set Nicodemus thinking. As the leading teacher of
our nation, he was very familiar with the
Law and its implications, and as a Pharisee
he recognized that the Books of Moses
were divinely inspired for all ages.

Jesus reminded Nicodemus of that incident on the journey to our land when our fathers sinned, and God judged them. Serpents bit them and large numbers died. Then, on instructions from God, Moses had a bronze model of a serpent made and lifted up a pole where everyone could see it.

"Look to the serpent and live!" Moses announced to the people. Strangely, those who looked were healed, and they lived. Those who did not look to the bronze serpent died.

Then Jesus said to Nicodemus, "Even as Moses lifted up the serpent in the wilderness, so must the Son of Man be lifted up." He had gone on to draw a parallel—that anyone looking to Him should have eternal life.

In recent weeks, after the crucifixion of the Christ, Nicodemus and I have talked about that discussion. Now he understands, but at first he did not. We now believe that some of those stories in the Scriptures, the historical records of our people, had a spiritual significance.

Actually that earlier visit by Nicodemus had a dramatic influence on his life, and it has helped me also. It will soon become clear that both Nicodemus and I proceeded from skepticism to belief and from cowardice to courage, as many people would express it.

As I said before, the cowardice is to be regretted, and we will never understand why we were so weak. The courage is quite easy to understand: we became convinced that Jesus really was the Christ of God. We did not understand all the theology, nor how the plan of God could be worked out, nor at the time of the crucifixion did we dare to hope that Jesus would be raised from the dead. However, we knew that somehow what had happened was ordained according to the overruling sovereignty of God.

I shall tell more about this later, when I write concerning the crucifixion of Jesus. For the moment, I want to tell you that my friend Nicodemus was convinced that Jesus was a true Prophet of God. In that nighttime talk, he even told Jesus that it was being acknowledged that He was a God-sent Teacher—for how else could these miracles be accomplished?

Looking back, it is indeed strange that more of us did not accept Jesus for all He claimed to be. How could anyone but the Light of the World give sight to the blind? How could the deaf hear at the command of a Man unless God was with Him? How could he order a widow's son to get up from

RABBI NICODEMUS MEETS JESUS AT NIGHT 25

his coffin, and be obeyed? How indeed, unless He be the Son of God.

Jesus told Nicodemus that rebirth was the activity of the Spirit of God. Men might not understand it, but, after all, they did not even understand the blowing of the wind. It was not really surprising if they did not understand the work of the Holy Spirit.

"How can these things be?" Nicodemus asked. He gave us quite a lot of details later.

It was then that Jesus said to Nicodemus, "You are the teacher of Israel, and you do not know these things?" He went on to point out that His own message with regard to earthly things was not listened to — so would men really listen to a revelation about heavenly things?

He told other profound things to Nicodemus, and my friend could not understand them at the time. One thought-provoking statement was something like this:

"No man has ascended to Heaven except the Son of Man who came down from heaven, and He is in heaven."

What did Jesus mean? After the crucifixion and resurrection we understood a lot better. Jesus was talking about Himself — in our Jewish writings we read a lot about "the Son of Man" and Jesus was taking that divine title to Himself.

That was not all. He was also claiming to have come from God. He was the Heaven-sent Man for whom we Jews had been searching for so long.

That last point that Jesus declared to Nicodemus had us thinking for quite awhile, but now we understood it somewhat better. Jesus was telling Nicodemus that He Himself was omnipresent. Apart from His putting His glory aside temporarily for our redemption, He was God, with all the attributes of Deity. Apart from His personal choice, He could not be contained in a Body, located only in one geographic location. He was on earth, and yet He was in heaven, at the right hand of the eternal majesty.

Jesus is God. As someone else has put it, "All the fullness of the Godhead is dwelling in His Body." Amazing, but true.

Looking back, we know it was *all* beautifully true. Nicodemus was right. Jesus was indeed a prophet sent from God. Our people are blind, and it is surprising. And yet, should we be surprised? We ourselves—Nicodemus and I—hesitated for so long, and it really took His death to bring us both out into the open.

Yes, and also His resurrection. Christ could not be held by death, so He rose again. We know it, for we walk with Him. We talk with Him, and we know that He hears our prayers. He is in truth the Teacher sent from God, the Son of God Himself.

Letter No. 4

Courage In A Den Of Thieves

At this point I must go aside, to give some important background, so that what follows can be better understood.

Right from the start of Jesus' public declarations, members of the Pharisee party had set out to expose Him. As one attempt failed, they would try another, but never successfully. Time after time they tried to entangle Him in His talk so that they could bring formal charges against Him, but not once did they cause Him to say a single thing on which a genuine charge could be laid.

For the Pharisees, my colleagues, this was frustrating, and eventually it was infuriating. They combined with the Sadducees to entrap Him, but still unsuccessfully. They even collaborated with the Herodians, whom they normally openly despised because they cooperated so willingly with the Romans.

On one occasion the groups came together and challenged Jesus: "Should we pay tribute to Caesar, or not?" Jesus knew they were trying to trap Him. If He said, "Yes," then they would hold He was denying His own claims to Kingship. If He said, "No," they could have had Him charged with treason against the Roman State. Jesus knew the implications, and He asked them for a coin. It bore the imprint of the Caesar, together with an inscription declaring the Caesar's divinity. Such coins could not even be offered in the Temple Treasury, for they were held to be endorsing blasphemy. Pilgrims had to change them into Jewish currency before making their offering.

"Whose is this image, and this superscription?" Jesus asked.

"Caesar's," they answered, not yet realizing that it was they who were being entangled, and not Jesus.

"Then render unto Caesar what is Caesar's, and unto God what is God's," He told them. They could not even offer Caesar's coins in the Temple to God, and Jesus had given them an answer that was masterly. Their plan had miscarried, and as those around Him smiled to themselves,

COURAGE IN A DEN OF THIEVES

my Pharisee colleagues silently gnashed their teeth.

There were other attempts to trick Him, as we have said, and they were all equally unsuccessful. Jesus could deal with a whole circle of opponents, and could quieten them one by one. His wisdom was itself another pointer to His more than human nature.

He was questioned about divorce, about the commandments of the Law, and even about life beyond the grave. Pharisees, Sadducees, lawyers, scribes—they all tried to entangle Him, but always unsuccessfully. Over and over again those who heard the exchanges declared such things as, "<u>Never did any other man speak as this Man speaks</u>." Constantly people were amazed at the masterly words that came from Him so naturally and graciously.

Those questions about tribute were especially relevant, for it was all part of a deliberate plan to discredit Jesus. The attempt was being made to trick Him into making a statement that could be construed as challenging the people to revolt against Rome. The leaders hoped to make the Romans responsible for the overthrow of Jesus, by forcing their hands to crucify a rebel and a leader of revolt.

Looking back, it seems incredible that more of us, the religious leaders, did not see things in better perspective. In self-justification I can only say we did not know all the facts. I am sure we would have acted differently if we had known what we now know.

For it has now become clear that the House of Annas (including the present High Priest, Caiaphas) was deeply involved in illegal practices associated with the Temple offerings. They were making a fortune out of the pilgrims who came long distances to bring their offerings to Jerusalem. Not only were they charging exorbitant exchange rates on Roman coins, but they were blatantly tricking the people in other ways.

One especially prevalent practice was relating to the actual offering of a lamb. A man would bring his little animal to Jerusalem at Passover time, but to his surprise he would be told by the priest that it had a blemish. The man would of course be terribly concerned, for he had come a long distance to make this offering. He would, therefore, be somewhat relieved to hear that fortunately the priest had another lamb which he was prepared to sell. So the pilgrim would hand over his own lamb and pay the high price for the special "lamb without blemish" which would be acceptable before the Lord, and then he would go his way.

As he proceeds out of the Temple precincts another man is coming in with his lamb. The act is repeated, with the first man's rejected lamb now being the one that "fortunately" the priest has available.

We now know that Annas and other members of his family were unscrupulous rogues. They had in fact turned the very Temple of God into a center of merchandise. Jesus openly referred to it as "a den of thieves," and His description was remarkably accurate.

We said we would turn aside to explain something because of its importance. All that we have said in this letter is highly relevant as to the reasons why, humanly speaking, Jesus was crucified. He was exposing the illegal practices of the High Priestly family.

Not once, not even twice, but three times He drove the traders out of the Temple precincts.

"Take these things out of here," He declared, "This place should not be a place of merchandise. You are making My Father's House a den of thieves!"

The first time was early in His public ministry, at the time of Passover, soon after He had begun to undertake miracles that showed He was the Son of God. There was a report that He had turned water into wine, and now He dared to expose the malpractices in the Temple precincts. There was immediate opposition from the High Priestly family, and a series of schemes began to be instituted against Him.

One by one those schemes came to nothing, and Annas and Caiaphas and the others were becoming increasingly frustrated.

Then came Passover week, still only a few months ago as I write this letter. Jesus came to Jerusalem, and stayed in Bethany at night, joining the pilgrims as they came into Jerusalem each day.

Actually two other events of special importance took place at that time: Jesus' triumphal entry into Jerusalem and the resurrection of Lazarus. I shall elaborate those in another letter, but at this time I want to deal with the incidents in the Temple. They are highly relevant as background to the trial of Jesus the Christ.

On two separate occasions, actually on successive days, Jesus came into Jeru-

COURAGE IN A DEN OF THIEVES

salem from Bethany and went to the Temple. On each occasion He quietly made a whip out of the pieces of rope that pilgrims had used to lead in their lambs to be offered.

When He had finished, it became quite an effective weapon as He drove the traders out from that sacred area, just as He had done on that previous occasion three years before. However, it was not only the whip that was effective: it was something about Himself: there always was that special something about Him Whom we call the Christ. When the soldiers went to arrest Him, they fell at His feet as though they were dead. On another occasion the High Priests arranged for Him to be captured, and He literally walked through the crowd and disappeared. Later I shall tell you about that hardened Roman centurion who watched the noble way He suffered on the Cross, then was heard to exclaim, "Surely this was the Son of God!" There was always something distinctive about Jesus the Christ.

So when He drove the traders out, it was not only the whip they feared but the reality of the Divine Presence active in their midst. The traders fled, fearful for their very lives.

Annas and Caiaphas were furious, for

this One was threatening the income from their lucrative malpractices. They were already rich, but in their greed they wanted more, much more. "This Jesus must be stopped," they declared, and they determined to end His work, by any means at their disposal.

They were interested parties to the trial of the Christ, for their sources of income were being challenged. The fact is, the whole trial was amazing.

Who were the witnesses? There were none found to agree among themselves. The trial should have been concluded without a conviction. Then Jesus was asked by <u>Caiaphas to testify against Himself, and this is illegal according to our judicial standards</u>.

"What need have we of any further witnesses?" Caiaphas demanded, and he tore his robe, signifying that Jesus was found guilty of blasphemy.

What were the charges against Him? They should have been properly laid before the witnesses gave their testimony, but they were never formally laid at all. It was only when Caiaphas declared Him guilty of blasphemy that there was any semblance of such a charge, and that signified the conclusion of this farcical "trial."

Then when He was brought before Pontius Pilate that "charge" was not presented, and Pilate was expected to put his seal on the execution sentence without any further investigation. Eventually yet another false charge was put forward—of Jesus wanting to be king instead of Caesar. It was as unsound legally as the Jewish "charge" had been. Two great systems of law had conspired to ensure the execution of a Man who had not been formally charged and had clearly been shown to be innocent of the wild and vindictive claims against Him.

Annas and Caiaphas should have been debarred from all participation in the case, for they themselves were involved in those illegal activities which Jesus had exposed. Instead they became accusers and judges, with enough influence and cunning to ensure that the Prisoner would be executed promptly, before an appeal could be effective and before there could be a successful uprising of the people on His behalf.

The fearless courage of Jesus had been demonstrated very clearly in that "den of thieves," and His actions were part of the reason why He was ultimately crucified. That was, of course, allowed of God for man's redemption. In the short run, the thieves appeared to triumph. In the long run, God's perfect plan was brought to its glorious consummation, for Jesus not only died, but He also rose again.

The final victory was His, and no thief could steal that from Him.

Another important happening occurred at about the same time as those incidents in the Temple. I refer to the Christ riding into Jerusalem on a donkey. I shall tell you about that in my next letter.

Letter No. 5

The King On A Donkey

One of the most impressive fulfillments of prophecy in the life of Jesus was on the occasion when He rode into Jerusalem on a donkey.

I did not personally see it, for I was in my own village of Arimathea at the time. I have talked to many people about it, and, like them, I am convinced that this is what the prophet Zechariah wrote about over 500 years ago. Clearly he was inspired by the Holy Spirit of God to describe the events of that day.

Jesus was staying much of the time at the home of Lazarus of Bethany. He had arrived there six days before the Passover and came into Jerusalem each day, just as other pilgrims did. He would come into the Temple, and He taught the Scriptures to many. The Chief Priests opposed this and, as we have said, they deeply resented His actions of overthrowing the money tables of those who were making exorbitant profits out of the Temple trading practices.

Jesus always knew that He Himself was the Central Theme of prophecy, and He was constantly alert to the fact that His whole life was lived according to a divine timetable. In ways I do not fully understand, He had veiled His glory, as we disciples now say. He deliberately allowed Himself to be limited in His knowledge. He became a true Man (but without sin) so that He could die as a Man.

Nevertheless Jesus meditated on the Scriptures constantly and always knew when a particular time had come.

So it was with His riding the donkey into Jerusalem. He knew that He must be offered to the people as Israel's King, and He also knew that He would be rejected. Prophecy was merely history written down before it happened, and so He knew He would do what was written, even though it involved His own death.

The time of His offering of Himself as King had come, so He sent two of the disciples with an instruction to go to the city, find a certain donkey, tell the owner that the Lord needed it, then bring it back for Jesus to ride into our Holy City. The

THE KING ON A DONKEY

disciples obeyed, and everything was fulfilled to the letter.

So Jesus mounted the donkey and began His foretold ride into the city, thronged as it was with pilgrims from far and wide. They were obeying our national tradition of coming to Jerusalem for the Passover whenever possible. Those pilgrims had heard of Jesus, and many had sat and listened to Him. Some had been healed by Him, and He was constantly a great Subject of discussion.

Now the cry went up ahead that Jesus the Messiah was coming on a donkey, entering the City through the Golden Gate. Was not this what Zechariah the Prophet had foretold? This was tantamount to a public declaration by Jesus, "I Am your King. I am the One to Whom Zechariah pointed."

The excitement was great, for many believed that the Romans would now be overthrown and the Throne of David would quickly be reestablished. The noise went ahead, and the increasing multitude was with one voice acclaiming the Son of David, Israel's rightful King.

"Hosanna," they kept shouting, "Hosanna to the Son of David! Blessed is the King of Israel Who comes in the Name of the Lord!"

Some cut down the branches of trees and put them down in the processional way, while others even threw down their coats and other garments. Many waved palm branches as they acclaimed the Son of David, even Jesus the Prophet from Nazareth in Galilee. The crowd was ready to do whatever their Messiah instructed them, and many fully expected that there would be an immediate uprising against the Romans.

They were wrong in those aspirations, for Jesus directed His opposition against the High Priests and not against the Romans. This was not the time for the putting aside of the Roman domination.

At the time some of the multitude were somewhat disappointed. They had expected more than the overturning of money-changers' tables and the driving of corrupt priestly merchants from the Temple. This highlighted one great misunderstanding of the mission of Jesus, for He had not come simply as a military leader or as a political revolutionary. His was primarily a spiritual power and His Kingdom was "not of this world." He had in fact come to die, and this was an unacceptable idea to many who looked for the

THE KING ON A DONKEY

Messiah.

Even Peter had once told the Lord that He should not talk of death, and Jesus addressed him as Satan—"Get behind me, Satan." If Peter had such a lack of understanding of the divine mission, it is not surprising that many in that rejoicing crowd also did not realize that their Messiah must die before His kingdom could be seen in its ultimate outworking.

Nevertheless, those who searched the Scriptures should have known that the Messiah would indeed die, even as Jesus Himself had announced. The very prophet who foresaw the King entering Jerusalem on a donkey also wrote that He would be sold for 30 pieces of silver, as happened at the hands of Judas Iscariot, and that the money would be cast to the potter. That also was fulfilled when the 30 pieces of silver were used to purchase the potter's field, to bury strangers in; he also wrote that His hands and feet would be pierced (as in crucifixion).

Not only did Jesus Himself fulfill prophecies, but others had contributions to make also, as with Judas the Betrayer, and the priests buying the potter's field.

Something else needs to be said about those crowds who acclaimed Jesus. In the main they were not the same people who demanded His crucifixion. Those people were stirred up by the High Priestly party and there were agitators there who could almost be regarded as professional troublemakers.

In fact, the Chief Priests had determined not to destroy Jesus at the time of the Passover festivities, for they feared the people. Large numbers of those people believed that Jesus was at least a prophet, and the priests were not anxious to be defeated because of public sympathy for Jesus.

When eventually the arrest *was* made, one reason for the unseemly haste, even to the point of illegality, was that it seemed probable that the pilgrims might well organize resistance, and perhaps even rescue Jesus. That was a major reason for the trial having been raced to a conclusion before any opposition could be organized. By the time many of the pilgrims had entered Jerusalem for that day, Jesus had already been taken away to be crucified. The whole procedure was almost incredible, and totally out of keeping with Hebrew concepts of justice.

Jesus rode into Jerusalem on a donkey, demonstrating humility and clearly fulfilling a well-known Messianic prophecy. The "common people" acclaimed Him, but the rulers rejected Him. They would not yield sovereignty to Him: the necessary transformations in their lives were unacceptable. Instead, they rejected the One Who was clearly foretold and ordained as their rightful King.

Letter No. 6

The Plot Against Lazarus

We have said that the High Priestly party resented Jesus' actions when He overthrew the tables of the money changers in the Temple. They also did their utmost to have Jesus condemned at a time when public sympathy would not be at a high pitch.

Yet another dastardly plan was against Lazarus of Bethany. Jesus had undertaken many miracles, such as healing the lame and giving sight to the blind. Then, not long before He was crucified, He restored His friend Lazarus to life.

This was no ordinary death. On other occasions Jesus had raised the dead, but in the case of Lazarus, Jesus had deliberately stayed away from Bethany until there was no possibility of doubting that Lazarus really was dead. The sisters of Lazarus had sent a message, hoping that Jesus would come and heal their brother, as He had so many others. Instead of going to Bethany immediately, Jesus had delayed His visit for two days. By the time He got to Bethany, Lazarus had been dead for four days. One of his sisters even commented that by this time his body was decaying.

The fact is, that delay was deliberate on the part of Jesus. He was making it forever clear that He had the power of life and death, that even when a man's body was seeing corruption, Jesus could cry, "Lazarus, come forth!" He did that and the dead man did come forth, very much alive.

What greater evidence could be offered as to the genuineness of Jesus' claims to be Messiah and Son of God? The Chief Priests knew it, and so they deliberately conspired to put Lazarus to death. Many of our people were believing on Jesus because of Lazarus, and Annas and Caiaphas were furious. Lazarus was a living testimony to the truth of Jesus' claims: by merely being alive and seen of men, he was a constant witness to all men that Jesus was the Son of God. So they conspired to destroy Lazarus, as well as Jesus Himself.

Caiaphas, of course, had a plausible explanation for such a dastardly plan. He claimed that it was necessary for Jesus to

THE PLOT AGAINST LAZARUS

die, for it was more expedient for one man to die rather than that the whole nation should perish. This was illogical and untrue: Jesus was not a threat to the national security of Israel. His "threat" was against the hypocrisy and malpractice of the High Priests themselves.

Right or wrong the extension of the argument of Caiaphas was that people were believing in Jesus because of Lazarus, and so Lazarus also must die. If the High Priests had their way, all followers of Jesus would be ruthlessly destroyed. It was known that Jesus had a close friendship with Lazarus, and with his sisters Martha and Mary. Caiaphas tried to condemn them all by an old tactic sometimes called "guilt by association." The real reason is that Lazarus, simply by being alive, is a source of great embarrassment to these High Priests whose spiritual eyes are so tightly closed.

As a result of their evil machinations, Lazarus is not in the public eye as much as he might otherwise be. Nevertheless he is a true disciple of Jesus, and never hesitates to give honor to God for the restoration of his life.

An interesting thought about Lazarus is that his home was at Bethany at the time

Jesus was crucified, and Jesus spent much of those last days in his home. If the High Priests had really intended to ensure a fair trial for Jesus, which was their duty, they could have sent to Bethany and had Lazarus speak as a witness for the defense. Many of our people were present when Lazarus was raised from the dead, and some are still living close to Jerusalem, in nearby Bethany.

Why was Lazarus not called? Why were none of those who saw him raised from the dead called? The answer is obvious. Such evidence would have ensured the rejection of the case against Jesus, and that was not the intention of Annas and Caiaphas. They would be satisfied with nothing less than the death of their innocent Victim, the One Who was in fact the Son of God.

Letter No. 7

The Illegal Trial of Jesus

In this letter I want to outline some of the ways in which the trial of Jesus was illegal and also tell some things about the trial itself. We Jews are very careful to ensure that justice is not only done, but that there is no doubt before the world that it has been done. We insist that the accusation be very clearly stated, with a formal charge laid at the beginning of the trial. That was not done in the case of Jesus.

Secondly, we are very careful to ensure that there is adequate publicity given to the discussion as the trial proceeds. In the case of Jesus, everything was done at night, which itself was illegal, and there was no discussion of a public nature. This was in flagrant disregard of our traditions and institutions.

A third right for the accused person is that he shall have full freedom, but Jesus was bound, had no access to those who could have been the witnesses for His defense, and in many ways had no freedom whatever. He was arrested at nighttime in circumstances that were at least very unusual, was tried during the night, sentenced as a new day was ushered in, and rushed to the Roman Governor, who was coerced into reluctantly agreeing to deliver to crucifixion a Prisoner Whom he three times declared was innocent.

A fourth protection for the accused person is against dangers of errors in testimony, but in the case of Jesus this fundamental right was totally denied Him. A whole series of witnesses were sought to present a clear case against Him, but the witnesses could not agree. Even when it seemed that at last the High Priestly party had found two who did agree, in actual fact there were substantial differences in their testimony.

That leads to a further point of illegality. Our law insists that a man cannot be condemned to death based on words from his own mouth at his trial, but in the case of Jesus the High Priest put Him under oath and adjured Him by the Living God to declare if He was the Son of God. Jesus could not be silent at that point, for to be silent would be to deny His rightful claim to be indeed the very Son of God. When He did so acknowledge Who He was, the High Priest immediately declared that He was guilty of blasphemy.

The proceedings were amazing by any standard. The Judge was the chief witness against the Accused; he was also the prosecutor, and we have seen that he was in fact an interested party, in that Jesus had exposed the corrupt commercial practices associated with the Temple. The High Priestly family were deeply involved in those practices.

In actual fact, the trial of Jesus before our Hebrew people was in three parts. He had been brought in the middle of the night before Annas, who was no longer High Priest because the Romans had deposed him. No formal charge was laid, and he even demanded of Jesus to tell him about His doctrine and His disciples. He was attempting to have Jesus condemn Himself out of His Own mouth, and that itself is illegal. After that preliminary hearing, Annas had Jesus sent, still bound, to his son-in-law Caiaphas, who is technically the present High Priest. Some members of the local Sanhedrin were present, and the trial that proceeded was a great miscarriage of justice. No witnesses for the defense were called at all, the witnesses against the defense did not agree, and indeed the whole proceedings should not have taken place at night, because this was a trial for a Man's life, a capital offense and not a money offense. Our law precludes trial on such a case at night. <u>Indeed, even if the Accused had been found guilty, our legal standards are such that a full day must pass before the sentence can be carried out.</u> The members of the Sanhedrin are supposed to discuss the matter at great length, and even after their votes have been given, the matter is not ended there. A vote can later be changed in favor of the accused, but not against him. These are safeguards that are built in to our judicial system, but in the case of Jesus they were totally ignored. Clearly this was a premeditated murder, setting out to dispose of Jesus, merely under the guise of legal formality. That legal veneer was thin indeed.

It is interesting to notice in passing that Jesus Himself showed obvious knowledge of legal procedures, as when He asked the High Priest why he was asking Him about what He had done. Jesus replied that the High Priest should not be asking *Him,* but should be asking the witnesses. That was the point at which Jesus was struck, which is yet another illegal aspect in this greatest mockery of all times. At that point Jesus again rebuked the one who had so acted, quietly insisting that if He had spoken evil, then someone should bear witness to the evil, but if He had spoken well, He should not have been smitten. This was a challenge to produce proper witnesses who would bear witness to evil, but such witnesses were not produced.

I have said that some members of the local Jerusalem Sanhedrin were present there at this midnight trial. Then when Caiaphas managed to get a formal statement as dawn broke, the local Sanhedrin assembled with those members of the Great Sanhedrin who had been summoned during the night, and in just a matter of moments the whole thing was over. A formal statement was made by Caiaphas, and the declaration was given that this One was worthy of death. Neither Nicodemus nor I were present, for though they sent for us during the night, we did not reach Jerusalem until the sun was in the heavens. We were amazed to find that Jesus was *already* condemned and was about to be taken before Pilate.

The charges against Jesus were then changed. As far as the Hebrew trial was concerned, He was supposedly guilty of claiming that He would destroy the Temple. This itself was nonsense, for Jesus had merely said that if they destroyed the Temple, He would build it up again in three days, and it was clear that He was talking about the Temple of His Own Body. Even if He had been guilty of saying He could destroy the Temple and rebuild it in three days, this was no capital crime. It would mean that either He was all He claimed to be as the Son of God, with supernatural powers, or perhaps that He was mentally ill. It was clearly not a capital offense and was merely a pretense, a veneer to ensure that this One was disposed of.

Part of the charge was that Jesus claimed to be the Son of God, and so this was blasphemy. The charge was put into the mouth of Jesus as the Accused Person, and there was no attempt whatever to see if the claims of the Accused Person could in any way be substantiated. He had undertaken many miracles, had given sight to the blind and hearing to the deaf, He had caused the lame to walk and had even raised the dead. Some of those people should have been called as witnesses, but instead there was an untoward haste as Jesus was rushed to His execution. Indeed, Lazarus, who had been raised from the dead just a brief time previously, lived not far away at Bethany. He could have been produced as a witness, as could many of the Jews who lived in that area.

The fact is, our own Scriptures testify that the time would come when God would be manifested in human form. Our great prophet Isaiah said that the day would come when a Babe would be born who would be the Everlasting Father, the Prince of Peace, and he used a number of titles that could be attributed only to God Himself. We have always looked forward to a Messiah sent from God, One Who would be a heavenly figure, Who would yet be the Son of David. Our rulers knew all these things, but they ignored them. They had decided that Jesus was not the One for Whom they were searching, and they simply found a way of disposing of Him.

So when Jesus was brought before Pilate, there was not even a clearly formulated charge. The rulers knew that the statement that He had blasphemed would not be accepted by Pontius Pilate as sufficient reason to execute a man and that the Roman Governor would regard such a matter as something that the Jews themselves should settle. <u>However, our right to impose capital punishment had been taken from us,</u> and our leaders merely wanted the execution warrant signed by Pilate so that they could vent their fury on the innocent Son of God. They expected Pilate merely to give a formal assent to what they had already decided. However, Pilate was the representative of the Roman powers, and as such, he was personally responsible to ensure that justice at least appeared to have been done.

He demanded to know what the charge was against Jesus, and there was great confusion as one said this and another said that. Pilate even taunted the rulers by telling them to take Jesus and to judge Him according to their law, for it was clearly a matter of religion on which they were presenting Jesus as the Accused Person.

Pilate himself was greatly concerned when the Jews at last shouted that Jesus had represented Himself to be the Son of God. He took Jesus aside, as was his right, and made personal investigations of His claims. The more he talked to Jesus, the more Pilate was convinced that He was innocent, and he even wondered if there

THE ILLEGAL TRIAL OF JESUS

might not be some truth in His claims. His own wife had had a warning dream about Jesus and sent a message to Pilate to be sure to do nothing against this Prisoner. Pilate tried to rid himself of his own responsibility by sending Jesus off to Herod Antipas who happened to be in Jerusalem at the time, the argument being that as Jesus had undertaken His great works in Galilee (and Herod was responsible for administration in Galilee), the matter could be decided by Herod. The ruse did not work, of course, and Herod sent Jesus back to Pilate after having mocked Him. Herod expected Jesus to perform some great miracle before him, for all he wanted was entertainment, and he hoped that Jesus the Great Wonder Worker would give him that entertainment.

Jesus had not said a word in His Own <u>defense before Herod, no doubt remembering that this was the man who had so illegally had John the Baptist executed</u>. He did not deign to say a word when Herod wanted Him to perform some great wonder. Jesus despised Herod—His disciples say that on one occasion He even publicly referred to him as "that fox."

Herod had sent Jesus back to Pilate, and in the end Pilate delivered Jesus to execution because he heard shouts from the courtyard beneath him that if he let Jesus go he was not Caesar's friend. According to the Jewish accusers, Jesus had claimed to be a King, and here were these people claiming that they had no king but Caesar. It was all so farcical because they themselves objected so strongly to the rule of the Romans, and yet now they wanted Jesus killed because He, according to their claims, was not prepared to accept Caesar as king.

Pilate must have been cynically amused at such a state of affairs, but his own history was such that he dared not clash too openly with these Jewish leaders. He himself had been rebuked by Rome for some of his callous murders and unnecessary actions which so seriously provoked our people, and when he saw that he could not secure the release of Jesus, he eventually gave Him over to execution. He had even offered Barabbas, a murderer and a thief, to be released. He deliberately chose a notorious criminal at this time when the custom was to release a prisoner—he expected that they would choose Jesus, for surely the crime of Jesus was not in the same category as that of Barabbas. He had been amazed when the people had so vociferously cried for Barabbas rather than Jesus, but the High Priestly party had stirred them into this sort of action.

Pilate insisted that the inscription over Jesus' head be exactly as he had put it—"This is Jesus of Nazareth, the king of the Jews." Our people had insisted that the title should be changed to be merely that Jesus *said* He was the King, but on that point Pilate was adamant.

In my next letter I will write about the events leading up to the crucifixion.

Letter No. 8

I Walked Behind Jesus

I must put down some of my thoughts and recollections about the day Jesus died. I have already written about His trial and about Pilate's decision to hand Jesus over to be crucified. Despite His physical weakness after being brutally scourged, Jesus was ordered to carry His own cross to the place of execution, known as Golgotha, or the Place of a Skull. Tradition has it that Adam was buried there, but that is not likely to be true.

Jesus stumbled more than once, and I was wondering what I could do to make His awful task easier. I felt so helpless. What *can* an elderly man do against the might of Roman soldiers who are ready with their swords and spears? However, one of them saw that Jesus was seriously weakened by what He had already endured, and he took an unusual step. He made an old man, a visitor to Jerusalem, take one end of the cross for Jesus. Jesus smiled at that old man, and as they walked slowly along that crowded street I somehow sensed that the old man felt he was strangely privileged to help carry that cross. Now I know he was indeed privileged: that old man, Simon, has become a friend of mine, and he and his two sons have become zealous followers of Jesus the Christ.

At first I thought the Roman soldier was acting out of sympathy for Jesus, but I soon realized he had a different motive. He and his superiors knew that earlier that week Jesus had ridden into Jerusalem on a donkey, with thousands of pilgrims acclaiming Him as their expected Messiah. When the majority of those pilgrims came back into Jerusalem later that day, they would be shocked to find that their "Messiah" was already crucified. Even as we proceeded toward Golgotha it was not yet the third hour of the morning.

The soldiers knew that speed was important, so they would not allow Jesus to collapse on the way. That might bring forth leadership from within the crowd, with someone prepared to take his courage in both hands, out of sympathy for Jesus Who was at least a great Prophet. If one

I WALKED BEHIND JESUS

such leader emerged, others would follow and a riot could ensue. So it was that Simon was pressed into service, and the procession continued in an orderly fashion, but with the troops making it clear that they would not treat lightly any attempt to stop them carrying out their orders.

I continued to walk behind Jesus. I was not conspicuous, for some other members of the Sanhedrin were there too. Indeed, a few of the priests were actually inciting the crowd to mockery and derision as Jesus walked slowly along the dusty road. His face was bleeding, His back was so cut by the scourging that His skin was hardly visible, and the bough of thorns was still pressed deeply into His forehead.

"Son of God! Messiah!" They mocked Him. "Where is your power now? Why don't you save yourself?"

I am not sure whether Annas and Caiaphas were in the procession, but I do remember that they were at Golgotha. They looked somewhat like evil animals, leering maliciously as their Victim was subjected to humiliation, insults, and torture.

"That's the end of him," I overheard Annas say to Caiaphas. "Messiah indeed!"

At first I myself was confused. Difficult

thoughts were racing through my mind. If Jesus WAS the Messiah, as I certainly had believed, why had all this happened? If Jesus was indeed the Son of God, would God allow this to happen? Or perhaps God would yet intervene to deliver His Son. Was it possible that Jesus had endured what He had because He was fulfilling the prophecy of Isaiah, "He was wounded for our iniquities"? Was He suffering like this, somehow taking the penalty of sins in His Body? For Isaiah had also said, "By His stripes we are healed."

Had we all witnessed the actual fulfillment of those prophecies? If so, Jesus had now borne those stripes in His Body: He was indeed "wounded for our iniquities." What then would happen?

My thoughts raced on. Jesus was—and is—the Son of God. Therefore He cannot die. Whoever heard of God dying? God had allowed what we had witnessed. Jesus Himself had actually commanded—yes, commanded—those who arrested Him to let His disciples go. He submitted to arrest and even allowed Himself to be bound. I gather He even knew that the troops were coming to arrest Him, so He was aware that this was to be the time for these things to happen.

Clearly, He was in control of the whole situation in a remarkable way. That has been strangely true right through the whole of these proceedings. Annas knew it and so did Caiaphas. Pilate also gave the impression that he was uneasy, almost as though he was the one on trial, rather than the One before Him who claimed to be a King Whose kingdom was not of this world.

Jesus was in control—God had not forsaken Him—and now that Jesus *had* suffered, what next? Were we about to see some awe-inspiring, divine intervention? I earnestly hoped so and indeed was ready to accept such a happening.

Now we were ascending the slope of Golgotha. The soldiers were actively restricting the crowds from coming too close, for they were very aware of the possibility of a rescue attempt. I noticed that even some of the merchants had joined the procession—I recognized two or three whom I had often seen at their stalls. It seemed that the spectacle of a crucifixion was too good a diversion to miss. Even business and money-making could be put aside temporarily so that the agonies of these victims could be watched and even compared.

Now the procession stopped, and the

Romans went through certain formalities associated with execution by crucifixion.

While Jesus was standing there, silently praying, one of the soldiers read out the charges against the three who were about to die. The two thieves were described first, with straightforward statements of crimes that were recognized as meriting the death penalty.

It was different when it came to Jesus. There were no true crimes recorded against Him, but the charge sheet made it seem that He was the chief sinner, One who surely must be dispatched from the living as soon as possible, in such a way as to suffer for those offenses.

What then were the charges? As I remember it, they were as follows:

1. By His words He had incited men to destory the Temple of God in Jerusalem;
2. He had taught that He was more than man, blasphemously claiming to be equal with God Himself;
3. He had encouraged revolt against Rome by declaring that He was the true King of Israel—and that He was One ready to desecrate the holiest of religious sites—a blasphemer—an instigator of rebellion.

For those "crimes" Jesus was to die.

It was all so ridiculous—the Chief Priests had often been pleased to hear how the Zealots had embarrassed the Romans from time to time. When the even more radical group, the Sicarii, carried out their terrorist activities against the common enemy who ruled over us, the High Priests were even more delighted. Now Jesus was to die, officially because He had incited revolt against the Imperial Roman Empire. It was farcical—and terribly unjust.

The other two to be crucified were soon uttering screams of agony. They had begun to resist their captors when the crosses were laid on the ground, and the men themselves were thrown roughly down. Each of them had tried to get up and run, but it was a battle against hopeless conditions. Each was held by two strong Roman soldiers while a third lifted his mallet and began his fearsome task.

The nails used were nearly a hand span long, and as they were driven into the wrists and then into the ankles of the two men, their sufferings were intense. I understand their screams were heard inside the city itself.

It was all in great contrast to what we witnessed with Jesus. He made no effort to run. He stood for a moment, looking into heaven, still silently praying. Then He placed Himself on the cross, with great dignity actually taking that place, not needing to be forced as with the two thieves.

He closed His eyes for a moment as the nails began their dreadful task of tearing through His flesh, but not a sound escaped His lips. One of the soldiers actually paused for a moment, apparently almost awed at the dignity and courage he was witnessing.

Then the three crosses were each lifted bodily and hurled into the holes prepared for them. The thieves both screamed at the bone-shaking impact, but there was no such reaction from Jesus. He was silent, even as He had been silent before His accusers. He had spoken before them only when His answers and statements could help *them* to make right decisions. So far as His own defense was concerned He had indeed been as a sheep dumb before her shearers. That, of course, is yet another of our great prophet Isaiah's prophecies.

Amazingly, boos and shouts of derision filled the air as it was seen that Jesus was indeed crucified, really was suspended in the air with a known criminal on either side of Him. It was as though Jesus was the worst offender, so loud were the mocking and insulting cries that were leveled against Him. Once again, the priests and their supporters were the ones who took the most prominent part in the hypocritical mocking.

"Come down from the cross—then we'll believe you! You saved others—now save yourself!" they taunted Him.

I noticed Lazarus in the forefront of the crowd. Word had reached him at Bethany, and, like me, he felt helpless as he now stood with that small group of personal friends of Jesus.

As I saw him there, looking very strong and very much alive, I marveled at the hypocrisy of some I had so recently regarded as my friends. If they were sincere, they needed no more proof than the sight of that man from Bethany. Spiritually, their eyes were blind and their ears were deaf.

That made it all the more amazing to hear Jesus cry out from the cross, "Father . . . . " We who were His friends listened intently. We knew He was praying aloud, and, of course, we all knew about His wonderful life and example. Nevertheless we were surprised—every one of us—at what He now prayed:

"Father, forgive them. They do not know what they are doing."

At that moment I was carried away with emotion. I quietly wept, and others with me also wept. The life of Jesus had been a demonstration of God Himself living before men. Now in His death He continued to show the marvelous character He had always displayed. He had taught forgiveness, and now He practiced it, even as He was suffering the agonizing torture of crucifixion.

He showed His wonderful character in other ways as He was enduring that inhuman agony. He saw His earthly mother nearby, standing with John who had been so greatly beloved by Jesus. He called out from the cross to them both, instructing John to care for His mother as though she actually was his own mother. He also told Mary to look on John as though he was her own son. It was really quite beautiful to see how He considered others when He Himself was suffering so extremely.

Later, after Jesus had died, I watched as John took Mary by the arm and led her away. She went to his home from that day, accepting the dying wish of Jesus to do so.

In an earlier letter I referred to that

nighttime interview with Nicodemus. It was highly relevant, especially as we now stood together, part of the crowd who had gathered to watch that dreadful act of crucifixion. Suddenly Nicodemus turned to me, a strange look on his face.

"Joseph," he said, his voice muffled because of what was being enacted before our eyes, "Jesus told me, 'As Moses lifted up the serpent, so must the Son of Man be lifted up.' This is what He was talking about—He knew about this all the time!"

As I looked up at that central Figure, so nobly suffering the agonies of crucifixion, I too began to understand. I grasped the hand of Nicodemus. "He is indeed the Christ," I exclaimed. "He is in truth, the Son of God. Our belief has been right all the time!"

Nicodemus nodded, his eyes misty. "And He is dying for me. He's dying to give me life, dying so that I can be born again. That's what He meant when I talked to Him that night! Born again . . . when I am old . . . !"

Later, after the resurrection, we were to understand more. But already the significance of His death was beginning to be understood. Somehow, Jesus was the suffering Servant of Jehovah, obedient unto death.

The two thieves had also joined in the verbal abuse being hurled at Jesus. At first we had been sickened by their taunting insults as they had cursed at Him and shouted at Him to descend from the cross, saving Himself and them also. Obviously they knew of His miracles—so could not One Who gives sight to the blind, and even raise the dead, deliver them from the cross? Their shrieks and their insults were in stark contrast to Jesus, suffering physically even as intensely as they were, but in noble silence. Actually, of course, He suffered far more intensely. His was not only physical, for He was enduring the spiritual agony of being forsaken of God His Father as He became sin for us.

After a time the shrieks of the two thieves gave place to sustained groans, and muffled cries of agony. The drug they had been given was having some effect. Then, as if in a final desperate effort, one of the thieves again started to hurl abuse at Jesus. Below him many of my callous colleagues were still insulting Jesus, hypocritically urging Him, "Come down from the cross, and we will believe you!"

So the dying thief took up the taunt. "Save yourself and us! Come down from the cross . . . . " And the insults were flowing from his mouth.

Then came another voice, the voice of the other dying thief, but now dramatically different. When we talked about it later Nicodemus and I realized that he had been influenced by the bearing of Jesus, even as we had been.

"Don't you fear God?" he demanded. "We're dying, and we're getting what we deserve. But this Man is not guilty of any wrongdoing." He paused for a moment, then managed to lift his head, and to turn toward Jesus.

"Lord—remember me when you come into your kingdom!"

For a moment even the rulers and priests ceased from their insults as they waited to see what the reply would be. When it came, it was regal.

Jesus turned His head so that He looked straight into the eyes of that tormented man who was still looking imploringly in His direction. "This day," He said, "You will be with Me in Paradise!"

Soon I realized that a strange calm had settled on that man: he was now dramatically different from the other criminal. He was no longer screaming, not cursing, not mocking. His relationship with Jesus had given him peace in a most unlikely situation. His physical life was ending, but his eternal life had just begun. The man knew this was true, for the King of Kings had said so. Somehow, as I watched, I knew this was so. That dying thief no longer feared death as he had done just a short time ago. A word from Jesus had made all the difference.

But it is late. In my next letter I must tell about the strange happening in the heavens that day.

Letter No. 9

The Sun Was Darkened

We Jews consider it a great miracle that the sun stood still in the days of Joshua. Some of our leaders have rationalized it and tried to give a natural explanation, but I do not find a need to explain away miracles. I believe in God, and He is all-powerful. If He chooses to order the sun to stand still, it will do just that.

I am just as convinced that God's power was shown on the day Jesus died. The heavens obeyed the command of God, and darkness covered the land. The rocks were rent and the earth did quake—so much so that many graves were opened—and indeed some who had earlier died were later seen alive in Jerusalem.

Jesus had been crucified at the third hour, and He hung in silence for three hours, except for those times when He prayed for the forgiveness of His enemies, promised the repentant thief that he would be with Him in paradise, and made provision for His mother Mary.

Then, just at midday, at the height of the day, the sun was blotted out, and we were in the midst of complete darkness. It was frightening—and yet it was marvelous. None of us knew how long it would last, and many of the people crept away, picking their way to their own homes or to the homes of friends. They had never known darkness like this.

I say it was also marvelous, for I knew that it must be the work of God. The Romans had certainly not expected such a happening in the heat of the day, and of course they had made no preparation whatever to provide torches for lighting. In any case, they were as men stupefied. They always feared omens from the heavens, and they wondered if God was showing His displeasure at what they had done. They simply waited, hoping that soon this amazing phenomenon would pass away.

At one stage I heard the Centurion shouting to two of his men to stand next to the cross of Jesus, apparently to prevent any attempt to take Him down from the cross.

The minutes passed into hours. Above us

we could hear the screams of the thief who had not asked Jesus for help, cursing and swearing wildly, sometimes screaming with his agony. Man is seen at his greatest inhumanity when he stands by and refuses to help a fellow man in circumstances such as dying the agonizing death of crucifixion.

After some time I heard some of my colleagues muttering among themselves.

"It must be almost the ninth hour," I heard one of them say; "We must go to the Temple for the evening sacrifice." Even though I could not see, I sensed that he was balancing his hour glass to calculate that the hour was almost up.

This was the day of the Passover sacrifice, and that sacrifice was about to be made, precisely at the ninth hour, in the middle of the afternoon.

They moved off, clumsily bumping into some of those who were still standing there. I heard them apologize several times, until their voices were out of range.

Then I heard another voice—a voice filled with anguish such as I had never before heard. Jesus was crying out in the very words used at the commencement of one of the Psalms of David.

"My God! My God! Why hast Thou forsaken Me!"

Later I knew the answer. He was forsaken because in those three hours He had known what it was to become sin. He bore the penalty of sins in His own body, and the Holy God shut off His face from Him. Nor did He allow ghoulish men or even sympathizing friends to see Him, His Son, in the intensity of those hours of suffering. A veil was drawn across the sun.

Now the darkness was beginning to dispel, and I heard another cry from Jesus.

"I thirst!"

One of the soldiers ran to where there was some sour wine, soaked a piece of hyssop in it, then put it on his spear and handed it up to Jesus. Jesus put His lips to it, but immediately drew His head back.

Then immediately something happened that surprised me. It seemed that Jesus drew His body up straight and looked around at those beneath Him, now suddenly clearly visible in the restored daylight.

"Finished!" He cried. It was just one word, but it was a marvelous shout of triumph, of utter exultation.

Why had He cried, "I thirst"? Suddenly I knew. A flood of light burst on my soul, and I found myself warm, my body tingling, my heart and mind rejoicing before God.

THE SUN WAS DARKENED

Jesus knew that He was to suffer on that cross, a<u>nd He also knew that He was to be made the Song of the Drunkards</u>, even as t<u>he Psalmist had foretold</u>. Until that happened He could not dismiss His spirit, for the work was not yet complete, as it had been prophesied.

Little did that callous, mocking soldier realize that he was helping to fulfill prophecy. Sour wine was to him an ugly joke, an inhuman act of a degraded man. It<u> implied that the person receiving it was so drunk that he would not know the</u> difference. He was making Jesus the Song of the Drunkards.

So Jesus had cried, "I thirst." He did thirst, of course. The Psalmist had also written, "<u>My tongue cleaves to my jaws</u>." His thirst pointed to the physical agonies of crucifixion, when He suffered so that His visage was marred more than the face of any man, and His Body distorted so that His very bones were out of joint.

He thirsted also for the love of men—thirsted for the friendship and fellowship of even those who rejected Him, as well as of those who had believed in Him. And He thirsted for the restoration of fellowship with His Father, God. His thirst was very real, in both physical and spiritual realms.

So all the prophecies were now fulfilled. Soldiers had earlier cast lots for the beautiful coat that Mary had so lovingly made for Him. The soldiers had also fulfilled prophecy—"They cast lots for my vesture."

Now Jesus need suffer no longer. Hell had done its worst. Men had shown how far they could sink, so that they were unlike men in their actions against a fellow-Man. God Himself could again accept man back into fellowship. It was all there, in that victorious shout, "Finished!"

We watched exultantly, Nicodemus and I, and some of the other disciples who were still with us.

Once again Jesus lifted Himself, as though the nails were unable to withstand the power He had within. He lifted His face toward heaven and cried, "Father, into Thy hands I commend My spirit!"

It was no longer "My God," but "Father." He was no longer forsaken of God, but safe in His Father's keeping. For Jesus had left us. We saw His Body sag—and then hang utterly limp. We knew that He was dead. None could hurt Him any more—neither devil nor man. His work of atonement was forever finished. As the Psalmist said in yet another Psalm, He could now sit at His

THE SUN WAS DARKENED

Father's right hand, until His enemies were made His footstool.

We were not the only ones who were impressed by that One on the central cross. Another was the Roman Centurion in charge of the crucifixion. He was heard to exclaim aloud, "<u>Surely this was the Son of God!</u>" He had never before witnessed such sublime nobility and submission in suffering. Probably he also recognized the significance of the happenings in the very atmosphere. The coincidences were too great to be explained naturally, and that Roman Centurion was really expressing the thoughts of many who watched the Son of God in His agony that day.

What it must have been in the vaults of heaven—the Second Person of the Trinity, dying on a cross as though He was a human criminal! "Surely this IS (not WAS) the Son of God!" they might well have exclaimed. "How amazing is the love of God toward fallen man!"

But there was more to come—more unusual happenings. Even as I watched the enactment of this greatest moment in history, I was conscious of something else. There was a sudden rumbling, and then the earth was shaking violently beneath my feet. The earthquake was felt right through the city.

Later I learned something else. As the priests on duty were near the Holy Place, and the High Priest was about to move into the Holy of Holies to sprinkle the blood of the lamb that had just been slain, the curtain between the Holy Place and the Holy of Holies was split from the top to the bottom. This was actually witnessed and reported—it was not torn from the bottom upward, as men would necessarily have done. This was the hand of God.

Jesus had dismissed His spirit at the very moment of the Passover sacrifice, at the ninth hour. There was no longer any need for an animal's blood to be shed in anticipation of the offering of the Lamb of God. The way into the Holy of Holies was made open, at that very moment. Jesus the Christ, the Son of God, had kept the divinely foretold appointment, to the minute.

God in heaven had answered Jesus. He had thereby declared openly to the world that the Sacrifice of Jesus had been made and accepted. Man could now know forgiveness of sins because He, the sinless One, became sin for us. The Lamb of God had died to take away the sin of the world, even as John the Baptist had foretold.

THE SUN WAS DARKENED

Another prophecy was fulfilled as the Roman soldiers came to end the sufferings of the victims suspended on the crosses above them. The Roman custom is to break the person's legs. In this way there is no longer any support at all for the body, and the victim suffocates quickly. So they came and broke the legs of the two thieves, but when they saw that Jesus was already dead they did not follow their usual custom. Instead, one of them thrust a spear into Jesus' side. I watched as blood and water gushed forth, and I remembered yet another prophecy, "They shall look on Him they pierced."

Once again the soldiers did not know it, but they were fulfilling prophecy, for not a bone of the Messiah was to be broken. The Scripture was fulfilled even as they did *not* break His legs.

We could not understand it all, for Jesus was indeed dead. It seemed we could only understand a little at a time. I was like others of the disciples—we could only grasp that something that had been prophetically declared had actually come to pass. God was working. Of that there was no doubt, but there still were things we could not understand. Jesus had not only suffered, but He had actually died. We could not yet understand that . . . .

I knew someone must take action to ensure He had a decent burial, and then I remembered that my own tomb was nearby. Why not bury Jesus in *my* tomb?

Then a thrilling thought raced through my mind. What was it that our great prophet Isaiah had said in that beautiful yet tragic song about the Suffering Servant of Jehovah? "He made His grave with the wicked," Isaiah had written, "But He was with the rich in His death." Of all the disciples—I write in humility—I had the greatest claim to be "rich." God has prospered me in material things.

Like many of my people it is my desire to be buried near the Holy City, and I own a double burial tomb. It is very close to where Jesus was crucified.

I was the one to whom Isaiah was pointing! *I* was the privileged rich man, the one in whose tomb Jesus could lie! He had indeed died with the wicked, but He was to be "with the rich" in His death. It was my privilege to ensure the fulfillment of that prophecy.

With a determination and courage I had never known before, I set off to the Palace of Pilate. I would beg the Body of Jesus— and He would be buried in my tomb!

Strangely, I rejoiced. My former colleagues would despise me, would debar me from the Sanhedrin, and even put me out of the synagogue. What matter! I was going forth to identify myself with the crucified Christ.

As I marched steadily toward the governor's palace, my heart was actually singing. Somehow, God would be victorious and His ways would be seen to be perfect.

Letter No. 10

I Begged The Body of Jesus

My own part in the events surrounding the death and resurrection of Jesus were really minor, but nevertheless I was involved and I shall record it as I recall it.

I had done my best to make it clear that I did not endorse the illegal decisions that the Great Sanhedrin had made. I have a reputation as a just man, but clearly justice was not done in the case of Jesus.

I have said that it was not strictly a trial—either before the Sanhedrin *or* before Pontius Pilate. The incident before Herod was, of course, of no real importance, in that Pilate was merely trying to find a way to evade his own responsibility. He should have released Jesus when he declared Him to be innocent. There was no case for Herod to consider, even if it was genuinely within his jurisdiction—which it was not. There was not so much as a formal charge laid, let alone an argument as to whose jurisdiction was involved. If it was to do with the Temple, as the Sanhedrin at one point claimed, then Jerusalem was the place for the trial. If it related to a supposed revolt against Rome, then it was within Pilate's jurisdiction, not Herod's.

It is widely accepted that Pilate knew he had acted illegally, hastily, and out of self-interest. Some say he has had great regrets about the decision he made to deliver Jesus to execution by crucifixion.

I sensed this to be the case when I went to him after the crucifixion. Pilate seemed like a man who was dazed or under the influence of a drug, and that is not surprising. His own wife had been troubled in a dream and had taken a most unusual step of sending him a message in relation to a judicial matter.

"Do not have anything to do with that Man," she had urged. "I have been greatly troubled about Him in a dream."

Pilate was typical of many of his people. They believed in omens, and he had taken his wife's warning seriously. He even took various steps to secure the release of Jesus, but unavailingly.

Jesus Himself had greatly impressed Pilate. As was his right by law, he had taken his "Prisoner" aside and talked to Him privately. Jesus had explained that His Kingdom was not of this world, and Pilate had found himself strangely interested.

But our Jewish people had been stirred up by some of the members of the Sanhedrin—my own colleagues—and had cried out that Jesus had claimed to be equal with God. One might almost have expected Pilate to ridicule such a claim, and he probably would have with "ordinary" mortals. However, he made no mockery of Jesus "claim." In fact he was awed by His learning and answers and made even greater efforts to release Jesus.

The fact is, Pilate made a number of efforts to have Jesus released or to evade his own personal responsibility for the crucifixion, the only form of torture that would satisfy the blood-lust of my colleagues. He sent Jesus to Herod, claiming it was Herod's jurisdiction; he told my colleagues to judge Jesus according to their own Law; he even tried to be the impartial judge giving a decision of "Not Guilty;" and he offered the notorious Barabbas instead of Jesus the Christ. Some of us later considered it a strange coincidence that each of those offered was named "Jesus," and that "Barabbas" means "Son of a Father." Thus Pilate offered Jesus, son of a father, or Jesus, the Son of the Father, even His Father God.

Even when Pilate had Jesus scourged, it was possibly as a compromise. It seems he hoped that the spectacle of that physically broken man would cause even my vindictive colleagues to call a halt, and say "Enough!" But Pilate was wrong, and there was no mercy whatever shown by those who should set the world a pattern of mercy.

Then came those hours of amazing darkness, commencing at midday, in the hottest part of the day. It had all Jerusalem talking—Romans, Jews, and visitors alike. Pilate himself wondered at what was happening and could not rid himself of a great sense of depression at the terrible thing he had done. Were the darkness and the crucifixion linked? Then there was that earthquake, just as Jesus died. Was it an uncanny coincidence, or an Act of God?

Undoubtedly Pilate wondered, and *his* mind was not as closed as the minds of those who claimed to be looking for the Messiah of God. *They* were callously indifferent to the agonies Jesus was endur-

I BEGGED THE BODY OF JESUS

ing and some of them regarded the premature darkness as an unfortunate coincidence which spoiled their fuller enjoyment of the spectacle of Christ hanging in humility for all to see.

In my last letter I told of my resolve to beg the Body of Jesus, and I did what I could to have an audience with Pilate. This was not easy, for Pilate was not in the mood to be conciliatory with any Jewish official, myself included. He had insisted on his own wording for the superscription over the Cross of Jesus and had gained a moment of satisfaction at that assertion of his personal authority. Nevertheless, a black mood descended on him again, and at first he refused my request to see him.

I persisted, and let it be known that I had a request of compassion concerning the Prisoner Jesus. Possibly Pilate knew of my reputation for justice and righteousness, or possibly it was simply that he was terribly disturbed at what he had allowed that day. Whatever the reason, a soldier came out to conduct me into Pilate's presence.

"Sire," I began immediately, "I have come to beg of you the Body of Jesus, Whom you ordered to be crucified this morning."

Pilate looked at me, and I sensed he was very surprised, either at my unexpected interest or at the possibility that Jesus was already dead. Sometimes crucifixion victims lingered for three days in agony.

"You are making such a request too soon, Counsellor," he replied. "The Man was crucified only this morning. He cannot be taken down while he is still alive. You know that!"

"I know it Sire, but Jesus the Christ is already dead. Your own soldiers did not break His legs as they did the other two, for they know He is already dead."

Pilate seemed puzzled, and his eyes narrowed as he looked intently at me.

"Are you sure of your facts?" he demanded. "I am not a man to be trifled with. How could He be dead already?"

I took my courage in both hands. "Sire, before He died He told some of His followers that He would lay down His own life and that He Himself could take it to Himself again."

"Yes, but how do you know He has died? He might have swooned," Pilate insisted.

"We who were there heard Him cry out to God that He was commending His spirit

I BEGGED THE BODY OF JESUS

to God, Sire," I told the Procurator.
"Then He dismissed His Spirit—He died."

Pilate signaled to a soldier in attendance, and then ordered him to go to Golgotha and bring to him the centurian in charge of the crucifixion. He was to testify to Pilate whether the prisoner Jesus was dead or alive. The man went off quickly, and I withdrew discretely. After a brief time I saw the centurion entering the palace and then a messenger came out to me. Once again I was ushered into the presence of Pilate.

"Your Jesus is dead. You may take the corpse," Pilate said curtly as he bent over his desk, signing the order.

"Thank you, Sire," I answered. Then I took the document and moved quickly away. I wanted to complete my plans before my former colleagues could thwart me, perhaps even having Pilate change his mind.

I hurried back to Golgotha, the Place of a Skull, stopping only briefly to purchase some linen. The store was actually closed, but the owner was peering out the door, as though looking to see what next would happen. I managed to persuade him that my need was urgent, and I was quickly making my way back to Golgotha again.

Nicodemus was still there, and I showed him the document. Together we approached the centurion's deputy, the man in charge in the absence of the centurion. We had returned to the site quicker than the Roman officer.

"Sir," I said respectfully, "we have come to take away the Body of Jesus the Christ."

"You have come to what?" the man asked, hardly able to believe his ears. If that Body was removed unlawfully he himself might forfeit his life. He seemed ready to cut me down with his sword. After the events of that day he was in no mood for foolishness.

"We have come to take the body of Jesus Christ," I repeated as calmly as I could.

"Don't waste my time or you might find that my temper is short," he warned, his voice menacing.

I produced the parchment signed by Pilate, and immediately the man's attitude changed.

"As you say, Sir, as you say," he replied deferentially. "Septimus! Octavius!" He called out imperiously, and two Roman soldiers came to him at the double. "Take the Prisoner Jesus down from the cross and deliver the corpse to these two counsel-

I BEGGED THE BODY OF JESUS

lors," he instructed.

The soldiers looked at us curiously, but then turned and promptly began their task of removing the earth at the base of the cross. Then we helped them lift it out so that Jesus no longer was a Spectacle in the air, but was a limp Figure on the ground.

I saw that His Body was distorted, and His face was marred more than I thought any man's face could be marred. And yet somehow that face also conveyed deep peace—a strange tranquility that I could not then or now explain.

The other men had by now gone, but some of the women were still there, and they went with Nicodemus and me as we gently carried His Body to my own prepared tomb which was nearby. We laid His Body there, without fully preparing Him for burial, for we were anxious to have Him removed from the scornful gaze of some who were even then anxious to continue their mockery. We simply wrapped His Body in that piece of fine linen I had bought as I returned from my interview with Pilate.

The women came with us and took note of where we laid Him. Then they hurried off to find spices and ointments so that the Body could be attended in a way more befitting our respect and love. Nicodemus also helped in this matter, for he was able to procure a substantial mixture of myrrh and aloes.

Soon our work was completed and we stepped outside, leaving that beloved Body in the tomb I myself had expected to occupy one day. I rolled the stone along the groove outside, and it completely covered the face of the tomb itself. I felt sad as I stood back to see that all was in order. Behind that stone lay the One Whom so many of us had hoped would be the Great Deliverer of our people. Now it seemed it had all come to nought. As I say, I was sad. So were Nicodemus and the women. Some winter flowers were blooming in the garden surrounding us, but the One Whom we had thought was the Lord of Life was lying dead behind that stone. One of the women stifled a sob, and I too was close to tears.

Some of us came back the next day, and stayed awhile to see that nothing was disturbed. I was about to move away with my friend Rabbi Nicodemus, but suddenly we realized that my tomb was about to be the object of attention from others. We recognized some of those of the priestly

I BEGGED THE BODY OF JESUS 99

party now approaching, and we decided it would be wise to step aside and watch the proceedings. We knew they would do nothing to the Body of Jesus, for Sabbath had been ushered in, and they would not "defile" themselves by so much as putting a finger on His Body. No, there must be some other reason for this Sabbath day visit.

It did not take long for the reason to be clear. A small party of Roman soldiers was there, together with troops from the Temple, and now the Tomb where Jesus lay was sealed, to ensure that nobody could come and steal His Body.

Then the soldiers took up their place nearby as sentries, ready if necessary to kill anybody who tried to remove the Body—and they *would* have killed such a person, for if the Body was taken, they themselves might have forfeited their own lives.

Later Nicodemus and I learned that some of our colleagues had gone to Pilate and demanded that he order the sepulcher to be sealed, but Pilate had told them to organize it themselves. He gave them the minimum of assistance, and we had witnessed their activities.

Now the hour is late. Perhaps tomorrow

I shall write about the actual happenings at the time when Jesus came forth from His tomb—the tomb that had been mine.

Letter No. 11

Jesus Left The Tomb

Sleep was difficult for many of us in those dreadful hours while Jesus was in the tomb. I hardly slept at all the first night: my mind kept going over all those challenging events. I remembered the noble way Jesus conducted Himself at every point, and I found myself marveling at His dignity and composure. I marveled at His words, not only when on trial, but even on the cross.

Everything was quiet during the Sabbath, and His disciples were in a state of shock. I myself was hardly able to comprehend the truth that had enveloped us all like a dark cloud. Jesus was dead. I myself had helped to bury Him: what further proof did I need? None. And yet I found it hard to comprehend. I shared the shock with my new friends from Galilee . . . and with Nicodemus.

Then we began to hear strange words.

Words that were thrilling, and raised us to a point of hope, but of course that hope was quickly extinguished. Jesus was dead. We had witnessed the blood—and the water—that dreadful hole right into His body. It was of course senseless to hope, and yet . . . .

We all obeyed the Law and rested on the Sabbath, but even before dawn on the first day of the week some of the women brought the spices and ointments they had prepared. With loving intent they moved through the quiet darkness toward the tomb I had given to our rejected Messiah.

The last of the stars was bidding farewell to the day, and then the soft light of the sun began to diffuse the eastern sky. It was a beautiful sight, but none of that silent group so much as noticed it.

"He saved me from myself. I can never be the same again," Mary Magdalene said sadly. And from her heart rose a silent note of anguish. "How could He cleanse me and change me like He did if He is not sent from God?"

"He was sent from God. That we know, but we can only leave it all with Him. He knows the end from the beginning." Was it Salome who spoke? Later the women were not sure. Their own conversation did

JESUS LEFT THE TOMB

not seem to matter. Their hearts were full to overflowing, and they talked of His love, of His miracles, of His power, and of course, of His death. They could not understand it, but despite their tears their faith was still in the God of their Fathers. And, in ways they could not explain, in His Christ.

Suddenly the women sensed a new cause for alarm, for the earth was shaking beneath their feet. For several moments they swayed to and fro, unable to control themselves.

"What was it?" they asked, as with one voice, and then just as unitedly they themselves gave the answer.

"It was another earthquake!" Later they learned that it was possibly the after-effects of the earthquake that took place when Jesus died.

The earth was still again now, and they were able to move ahead, trembling it is true but still determined to complete their task of anointing His body. They each loved Him with a holy love they knew came from God.

"Look at the tomb!" Mary Magdalene pointed excitedly. "The stone has been rolled away!"

"Yes, and the Lord Himself is in our

midst!" I believe it was Salome who first expressed this great truth in words. She was right. The Angel of the Lord, the special messenger of God Himself, had descended to the earth and had indeed rolled back the stone. Now, as the women approached, they saw the magestic Angel of the Lord.

They also saw the keepers—shaking much more than the women, and with good cause! They had dared to set themselves up as the keepers of the body of the Son of God, to ensure that the seals of the tomb were not broken. Puny mortals! No wonder they trembled when they saw this One Whose very face was as bright as the lightning, with clothes gleaming white like snow.

Those keepers watched in terror.

"What is it?" They asked each other. "What can we do? How can we stop Him?"

The officer in charge knew he was expected to take a lead, but he could do nothing. He was as terrified as the others now prostrate on the ground.

"He's a Son of God!" He exclaimed hoarsely. "A messenger from God Himself. What have we done!"

"Quiet man, or we'll all be dead!" It was one of his subordinates who spoke,

JESUS LEFT THE TOMB

"And cover your face if you want to preserve your eyesight!"

The officer of the guard meekly obeyed, and for several minutes there was silence. Later they accepted bribes and declared that they themselves had slept, and that some of the disciples came and stole the Body. Nonsense. They did not sleep, even though they were lying on the ground. They were more like dead men—dead of fright.

The women were also terrified at first, but they did not fall to the ground.

"Who are you, my Lord?" they asked, perplexed. This was an unexpected development. In the gathering light they could now see that the tomb was open, for the stone had been rolled away.

"Fear not," the Angel of the Lord answered. "I know that you are looking for Jesus Who was crucified. He is not here, for He is now risen, just as He said He would rise. Come and see the place where the Lord lay."

Here was this heavenly messenger referring to Jesus as "the Lord." And with commanding authority He was beckoning the women forward so that they could see for themselves that Christ was indeed risen.

"See—that is the place where He lay."
Each of the women stepped inside. As they explained it to us later, their minds were full of wonder and of exultation. They knew that God had worked.

"I am the Resurrection and the Life," they remembered Jesus saying at the grave of Lazarus. "If you will believe, you will see the Kingdom of God," He had declared on another occasion. And yet again, "Why did you doubt, O you of little faith!"

And the Angel of the Lord! Had not an angelic messenger appeared to Abraham, and to Joshua, to Gideon and to Manoah and his wife in Old Testament days? God was at work, and Jesus was risen! Risen? But that could not be. They too had seen the blood flow from His side . . . had watched that beloved body sag in death after declaring that He was committing His spirit to His Father in Heaven.

There must be some other explanation. They were confused, perplexed, unsure of themselves and of the events around them. If Jesus was risen, where was He? They had come wondering how to roll the stone away, and had arrived at the very time of the earthquake. That was when the stone *was* rolled away. Where then was Jesus? His body was not in this empty tomb, but

JESUS LEFT THE TOMB

where was He?

"Where can He be?" Salome asked, almost to herself.

"Yes indeed—what shall we do? Who would have taken Him away?"

Hope was beating in the heart of Mary of Bethany, for she too had gone with that company of women. Several of them were there, for mutual protection. Normally they would not have done such a thing, for it certainly is not safe these days for women to be alone on the streets when there are not large numbers around. Probably they would have been wiser to have asked the men to go with them, but that is the difference between women and men. They wanted to express their love at the first possible moment and to anoint His body with the spices and ointments they had so lovingly prepared.

So they had quietly talked together and arranged their early morning program. Mary Magdalene went along. She had so much to love Him for, and her sorrow was great, yet it was beautiful. She was a transformed woman, with the power of her new life still showing through her tear-filled eyes.

Joanna, and Mary the mother of James, were also there. So was Salome, and several others. As I said, I believe there was also Mary of Bethany, together with quite a group of faithful keepers. Some of our friends who were closer to those early disciples could tell you the other names.

I must get on with my account of that morning. So much happened in a short time that it is not easy to give you the whole story in precise detail. I think it would be best if I reconstructed it as I believe the events of those few minutes took place, though others might want to correct me at one point or another.

Inside the tomb the women noticed the coverings of Jesus' body, neatly placed where He had lain. There was the head-covering, and over here was the linen garment, stained with His blood, a lasting testimony to the reality of His sufferings. Perhaps that shroud should be kept as a memorial of His time in my tomb.

"Who are you looking for—for Jesus of Nazareth?" It was a kindly voice, and suddenly the women realized they were not alone. They had crowded into that large double tomb area, uncompleted as it was, and now they realized there was a young man sitting there. In the confusion they had not noticed him. This was not surprising, for they had stepped from the soft light of breaking day into the darkness of a tomb cut in the rock. Some of the women did not even notice that a second angel, for such they were, was also sitting there. In their state of near-shock and sorrow, it was not at all surprising that they did not take in every detail of the scene before them in that gloomy interior.

One of the men in shining garments gently asked, "Why do you look for the living in a place put aside for the dead? He is not here. Don't you remember what He told you when He was with you in Galilee?"

The women from Galilee especially remembered that. Yes indeed, Jesus *had* clearly told them He would die, but also that He would rise again.

The angel was going on. "Don't you remember that He said that the Son of Man must be delivered into the hands of sinful men, and be crucified, and rise again on the third day?"

Yes, the women *did* remember. They remembered all this and much more. As Samaritans, they kept the Passover from morning to morning, and not from evening to evening, as the Judeans did, and they knew that Jesus had partaken of the Passover Supper with the men according to their own established timetable.

"And He died at the very moment when we Judeans began our evening sacrifice—at the ninth hour!" I believe it was Mary of Bethany who suddenly saw the double significance of the two suppers. Jesus had died as the Passover Lamb, keeping a divine appointment to the very minute . . . and now He had risen from the tomb, again at the very moment of God's appointment! It was at the time of the sun's first appearing, when the earthquake was felt by them all—and the stone was rolled away! Jesus was not to stay in the tomb once the first day of the week had broken.

So it is true—Christ is risen!

They listened again as the angel went on, "Now you go on your way. Go to His disciples. Go to Peter. Tell them that Christ is risen, and that He is going before you into Galilee. You shall see Him there, even as He told you."

In the young light of that morning a casual observer would have been surprised to see a large group of women hurrying back inside the city's walls, and in the front of the group were three women running. Mary Magdalene, Joanna, and Mary the mother of James found themselves with an energy they had not known in years. They

JESUS LEFT THE TOMB

ran all the way to the home of Mark where a number of the disciples were staying.

"The Lord is risen! The Lord is risen! The tomb is empty!" they cried, their excitement great. "An angel rolled back the stone during an earthquake—and He told us the Lord is risen!"

"They're in a state of shock. That's how it affects women. They can't take things like us men," one of the disciples said quietly, and several others took it up. It was clear they were not taking the women seriously. Their words seemed to the men as idle tales.

However, the women were persistent. "I tell you, the tomb is empty. At least we are sure of that," Mary Magdalene exclaimed, her voice breaking emotionally. "His body is gone, and we don't know where they have laid Him." She herself was confused now, disturbed by the disciples' unbelief.

She looked pleadingly at John, and then at Peter.

"Peter," she said solemnly. "That is not all. The angel mentioned you by name. He told us to tell the disciples, and then he especially referred to you."

The eyes of Mary Magdalene were full of pleading as she looked into the eyes of the man who had been Jesus' special assistant, a leader who was ready to act whenever Jesus spoke. Peter remembered another time, only three days ago, when he had been looked at in a special way, and without another word he got up and went outside. Now he started to run toward that rock tomb, my tomb. Jesus' tomb.

Peter was full of hope, yet he was also confused, as he did not yet fully understand the Scripture that Christ must rise from the tomb. His flickering faith was beginning to hope against hope.

John drew alongside, for he too had been impressed by Mary Magdalene's earnestness. For a little distance they ran together, but then John outran Peter and got to the tomb first. John did not actually go in, but he stopped at the entrance and looked inside. He could see it was empty, with the clothes lying just as Mary Magdalene and the other women had declared.

Now Peter arrived at the tomb and gently pushed John aside so that he himself could enter the tomb. There was the headdress—and over here was the linen garment . . . but Jesus Himself was not in the tomb. He was risen!

So Peter and the others must go to Galilee, even as they had been instructed.

JESUS LEFT THE TOMB

Now Peter and John and others who had followed, went back to the house to prepare for the journey home. The Lord was risen! The Lord was risen! Soon they would see Him again in Galilee!

There was renewed joy—yet still some nagging doubts. Had someone stolen the body? If only they could see Him in His Person!

Mary Magdalene had followed Peter and John back to the tomb. As they left to return to the house, she stayed outside the tomb, quietly weeping. She was confused now. What *should* she believe? It had seemed so clear, and then the men had been so full of doubts. Where was her Lord? How did His body go straight through those grave clothes without disturbing them? Where was He? If only she could see Him! And she wept.

She came back to the outside of the tomb, and again looked inside. She wiped some of the tears away, and now she could see the two angels, again sitting there. One was at the feet and the other at the head where the body of Jesus had lain.

"Why are you weeping?" they asked her.

"Because they have taken away my

Lord, and I don't know where they have laid Him," she said, weeping again.

She turned around and through her tears she saw another figure, a Man, standing there. She supposed He was the gardener, not knowing that in fact it was the Lord Himself.

"Woman, why are you weeping?" He asked gently. "Who are you looking for?"

Mary could not control her sobbing.

"Oh sir," she pleaded, "If you have carried Him away from here, tell me where you have lain Him, and I will take Him away!"

Mary knew all too well that the Jews would want to throw her Lord's body onto Gehenna, the burning fires for the rubbish of the city. That must be prevented at all costs. That little woman really meant that she personally would carry His beloved body to safety.

Jesus said only one word.

"Mary!"

Suddenly blackness was turned to light, sorrow to joy, anguish to ecstasy.

"My Lord! My own Lord!" she exclaimed, coming toward Him, to worship Him.

"Don't touch me, Mary. I am not yet ascended to My Father. Go to my brethren, and tell them that I am ascending to My

JESUS LEFT THE TOMB

Father, and to your Father, and to My God Who is also your God."

Some of the other women had rejoined Mary now, and they grasped the Lord by His feet.

"No," He said gently. "Do not touch me at this time." When they talked about it later they realized that Jesus must first ascend to God as the firstfruits of the resurrection. He was their great High Priest, presenting Himself "to My God and to your God." His blood had been shed, and now the way into the Holy of Holies was opened for all.

So the women returned to the house, and joyfully shared with the other disciples all that had happened early on that wonderful first day of the week.

Those women knew they had met the Lord, and yet He was changed. They had been there when the earthquake happened, and had actually been near as the angel rolled back the stone. Yet Jesus was not there. He was no longer in the tomb. He had immediately removed Himself from the interior, for the break of day signaled the end of His appointed time in that place. He did not need angelic help to remove Himself.

Jesus had laid down His life, as He said

He would, and He had taken it to Himself again and had come forth quite unaided. The rolling back of the stone from the empty tomb was for the disciples to see and not to release Jesus.

It was indeed Jesus Himself Who rose from the dead, for I myself, Joseph of Arimathea, saw Him, as did hundreds of others. Yet He was no longer limited, as He had been before His crucifixion. He could walk through closed doors and could even walk several miles to the village of Emmaus on those nail-pierced feet. On that road He revealed Himself to two of the disciples, and He is indeed the same physical Person, really flesh and bones. However, He has thrown off the restricting bonds by which He had veiled His glory before He died.

I have been accused of stealing His body, and it was alleged He did not really rise from the tomb, but that is nonsense. Because He rose, thousands have become courageous followers where previously they had not dared to announce their allegiance to Him. There were no other men besides Nicodemus and me at the tomb when we placed Him there, but now large numbers of men (as well as women) have come out openly to declare themselves as followers of the resurrected Christ. One especially pleasing feature to Nicodemus and me is that many of the priests are convinced by the evidence and are now true believers and followers. They have, of course, been put out of the Synagogue.

One other point seems insignificant, but I shall mention it. I said that when Jesus rose from the dead He left behind that linen shroud which I personally, with Nicodemus, had wound around His body. We had first covered Him with it when we took His Body from the cross, to avoid undesirable attention from ghoulish onlookers. At that time the blood was yet fresh, and even the bough of thorns was still penetrating His forehead. We removed that ourselves and covered His head also with the shroud.

Now I have found that there is some strange quality about that linen covering. It is almost as though it is a painting, or a life impression of our Lord's Body after He had suffered. As the tomb is legally mine, I suppose the shroud is also. I shall certainly see that it is hidden in a safe place. Nevertheless it worries me somewhat that this same shroud could be an object of worship, and I'm sure that would not be pleasing to God. I remember that our fathers were rebuked when they worshipped the bronze serpent after those incidents in the wilderness. It is entirely likely that some weak followers would also worship this shroud. By hiding it I believe such a possibility will be avoided.

There are, of course, all sorts of criticisms about the resurrection of Christ. Nevertheless, even apart from our own convictions, the evidence is overwhelming to demonstrate that Christ is indeed risen. Peter and all the Apostles saw Him and talked with Him, and so also did our Lord's own half-brother, James. On one occasion, hundreds of us saw Him at one time.

He has eaten food, and He has allowed the wounds in His wrists and feet to be seen. On one occasion He even told Thomas to put his fingers into the wound marks left by the crucifixion. Among the disciples it is known that Thomas is not easily convinced, but on that occasion he became convinced that Jesus was indeed his Lord and his God.

There is more, much more. His intimate disciples have undertaken miracles in the Name of Jesus, and many of the priests have become convinced because of the fulfillment of Old Testament prophecies about the Messiah's death and resurrection. They had not known the meaning of these prophecies before, but now they marvel that they were blind for so long.

The disciples themselves have become courageous, where before they were weak, and even I, an elderly man, have suddenly found myself utterly committed to the cause of the resurrected Christ.

As so many of my friends say, "Christ is risen. Hallelujah!" I know it is true. Praise God, my tomb is now empty, a mere cutting in the rock.

Letter No. 12

The Resurrection Of Jesus The Christ

In this letter I want to write again about the resurrection of Jesus. My former colleagues have made all sorts of ridiculous statements, and in this letter I want to make it clear that those stories are quite unacceptable. It is very clear from our own Jewish Scriptures that the resurrection of Jesus Christ should be expected by all those who wait for the fulfillment of our prophecies. Jesus Himself was questioned by the Sadducees who do not believe in a life after death, and in His reply He chided them for not knowing their scriptures well enough, then pointed out that God said, "I *am* the God of Abraham, Isaac, and Jacob;" the implication being that God is the God of *living* people. Therefore Abraham, Isaac, and Jacob are *alive* in the presence of God. The Pharisees believe in the resurrection of the dead, and in fact this is an area where it is known that the Pharisees and the Sadducees have a typical difference of belief.

Our Old Testament prophets pointed toward a resurrection, for did not the mighty Isaiah state in his Scroll that the dead would live and that their corpses would rise? Daniel also spoke of the resurrection of those who had passed on to everlasting life, or to a state of everlasting distress. Then, too, the Psalms state that <u>our Messiah would be resurrected, especially in that wonderful sixteenth Psalm</u>. The disciples of Christ have made it clear that they recognize that Jesus looked on and spoke about the resurrection. Other great men such as Isaiah, and of course Job, and indeed Hosea and Ezekiel, also spoke about that coming day when men would live on in the presence of God.

The disciples have constantly made it clear that Jesus Himself predicted that He would die, and that He even stated that he would die by crucifixion and rise again on the third day. The fact is, Jesus did die, and He was buried in my own prepared tomb, and that tomb was sealed—not by myself and Nicodemus, but by the Roman

THE RESURRECTION OF JESUS THE CHRIST 123

authorities at the specific request of the Jewish leaders themselves.

A sentry was placed to see that nobody came to steal the body, but on the first day of the week at that memorable Passover time, Jesus rose from the dead. He was seen alive by large numbers of disciples and by individuals who were His close associates for nearly six weeks—forty days, to be exact. His resurrection was witnessed by so many reputable people that it cannot be other than accepted if people are to be unbiased in their consideration of this wonderful subject. He fulfilled the Old Testament Scriptures, and indeed Old Testament types, and then the Holy Spirit of God was poured out upon the believers.

In one of his speeches, Simon Peter made it clear that God had anointed Jesus of Nazareth with the Holy Spirit and with power, and that power was transmitted to His waiting church—they were waiting in Jerusalem for that experience we have begun to call the Pentecost experience, just as Jesus had told them to do. That gave the church a new power, and even miraculous activities have been undertaken by some of those who were especially chosen by the Lord to be His witnesses after His resurrection.

The truth of the matter is that the resurrection of Jesus is an unassailable fact. Just as the Jewish leaders had done their best to find false witnesses against Jesus at the time of His trial, so they did their utmost to quieten those who declared that Christ was risen from the dead and that the tomb was empty. They paid money to silence the witnesses, and put out the story that the disciples had come during the night to steal the body.

It is relevant to ask how they would know that? There is no evidence whatever of a confession to that effect by any who were believers in Jesus as the Christ, and as you meditate upon this even that point of evidence becomes a telling witness against those who perpetrated the story. The Jewish leaders were determined to deny that resurrection, and their method was to grasp at any story, no matter how unconvincing. If the guards were awake they would not have *allowed* the body to be stolen, and if they had been asleep they would not *know* that it had been stolen. This, as I say, is a story that is quite unsupportable.

Of course the Jewish authorities tried to get around it by stating that the soldiers had been bribed, but even if that were true (and they were bribed, but by the *Jewish leaders* to support their story), this would immediately destroy the witness of those Roman guards, for by the standards of evidence accepted by our Hebrew people and the Romans, once bribery has been admitted the testimony of that witness is no longer acceptable. The penalty for falling asleep at the post was death for a Roman soldier, and the more we study this supposed falling asleep and the stealing of the body, the more we are satisfied even on purely legal grounds that it is a great concoction.

If the disciples had stolen the Body, it would have been relatively easy to institute a search and to find out where the Body was. The resurrection of the Lord Jesus Christ is an established fact. I know, for I was among those who saw Him alive. I who gave my tomb to be a resting place for the Son of God, saw Him alive, risen from the dead, victorious over sin and death and hell. Jesus rose from the dead, and He is still alive, and His power is known to those who follow Him.

This was not merely a spiritual phenomenon, for it was literal and physical: the Lord Himself made that clear. One of His disciples—to be specific it was

Thomas—actually doubted whether Jesus had risen, because he was not there when the Lord first appeared to the disciples. Later Jesus again appeared before that intimate group and told Thomas to put forth his hand and to feel the wound marks in His body. Thomas was totally convinced, and his friends say that he immediately declared, "My Lord and my God!"

Of course there have been arguments put forth against the resurrection. It has been stated that if the resurrection really occurred, this would have been a happening that was unique in all of history, different from the mythologies of ancient peoples—but of course it is unique, for this was the foretold resurrection of the Son of God. This was the miraculous intervention of God at the appointed time.

This was not simply Someone who had revived after being in a swoon for some days, for Jesus revealed Himself to two of the disciples in a long walk to Emmaus, several miles from Jerusalem. Despite the wounds in His feet, He walked without any apparent difficulty. His sufferings were past.

This was no basic falsehood, but the wonderful fulfillment of the promise of God, a promise which led to dramatic changes in the whole personality of men. Peter is a good example—I have already said that he denied his Lord several times while Jesus was being tried by Caiaphas and the others with him, (I was absent at that time). Peter denied his Lord, but as a result of the resurrection Peter was changed, even telling the Jewish leaders that they had been guilty of the murder of Jesus, their Christ. Peter was dramatically changed because Christ had risen from the dead.

All this is very relevant when we consider the claims of the authorities that the disciples had stolen the body. It is incredible that they would show such courage, challenging the might of Rome as well as the hatred of the Jewish rulers, in a way that simply was not demonstrated at the time of Jesus' trial. Not only would such courage have been out of character for the disciples, but to have then foisted such an incredible hoax on the world—and be prepared to *die* for it—is, of course, total nonsense.

Those disciples who were closest to the Lord had their own contentions and disagreements at times, and there are honest records about that. It is simply not to be taken seriously that they might have unanimously agreed on such a hoax, concocting evidence to show that they had seen the Lord, and then going out prepared to die for it. Such a claim does not merit serious consideration, even though that argument is being put forward by men who are determined to discredit this amazing resurrection at any cost.

Some are claiming that the Romans actually removed the body, but of course if Pilate had arranged for this he would have informed the Jews in order to put an end to this strange teaching about the resurrection. That would have shown once and for all that the preaching about the resurrected Christ was without historical foundation. There could be no motive for the Romans to deliberately arrange for that body to be stolen. This is just another story my former colleagues are grasping at so they can continue to reject the fact that the resurrection actually did occur.

The fact is, Jesus was buried in the tomb that was being prepared for my own eventual resting place. As I have already shown in an earlier letter, his body was prepared for burial in the way that is normal to us Jewish people. Various reputable women saw the tomb and looked inside to see where Jesus had been laid. I myself bear witness that the facts are as

THE RESURRECTION OF JESUS THE CHRIST 129

they have been commonly reported among the disciples.

I have been surprised to find that some even claimed that I myself either stole the Body or had it removed. This is nonsense and would totally oppose my own moral standards. Assessed from a sensible point of view, it again becomes clear that neither I nor any other person could have stolen that Body under the eyes of the Roman guards, men who knew that their lives would be forfeited if that seal was broken and the body removed.

Let me state that to identify with Jesus in His resurrection has cost me greatly. I have incurred the contempt of those who were my close associates, my life is in danger from the leading members of our priesthood, and I have known what it is to be ridiculed for identifying myself with One Whom they declared was discredited as a prophet of God. I have gladly accepted those consequences, because I am totally convinced as to the resurrection of the Lord Jesus the Christ. I listened to Him, I saw Him, and I know that the One Whom I saw alive was the One Who was buried for some days in my tomb.

Despite the ridiculous arguments that have been raised by those who were my former colleagues, the historical fact is that Jesus died, was buried, and rose again — just as the prophets of our Scriptures had foretold.

Letter No. 13

"Don't Fight Against God!"

A few days ago I had a long talk with Rabbi Gamaliel. He is not himself. He still has the respect of our leaders, but he confessed to me that he is very uneasy about the continuing interest in the Way.

"What if Jesus was the Christ?" he said in almost a whisper. "If he was, then I gave my vote against the anointed of God!"

I nodded. "You did just that," I told him very seriously. "You have done a terrible thing, Rabbi. You should confess your sin and ask God's forgiveness."

"If Jesus was the Christ, surely there can be no forgiveness?" Gamaliel insisted. "My sin would be greater than that of the despicable traitor, that Judas Iscariot."

"The amazing thing is that God *can* forgive you," I assured him. "You're one of those for whom Jesus cried out from the cross, 'Father, forgive them, for they do not

131

know what they are doing.' God can forgive to the uttermost all who come and ask for it. But they must come."

"I'm still not sure," Gamaliel answered. "My colleagues remind me that no prophet ever came from Galilee, but then I remember what the great Isaiah wrote—that Galilee would see a great light. When I think of that I remember that Jesus said, 'I am the Light of the World.' The way this movement is spreading, He might indeed be the light of the world."

Not much more was said, but it was obvious to me that Gamaliel was at least half convinced that Jesus was all He had claimed to be. Possibly we shall see a great movement among the priests, for they of all people must know that the Old Testament pointed to just such a One as Jesus of Nazareth.

That conversation took place several days ago, and now there has been a new development. Many signs and wonders have been done by the Apostles, and because of this and their preaching about Jesus, a whole group of them were thrown into prison. However, the Angel of the Lord opened the gates of the prison, and the disciples were all released. They were told by the Angel to go to the Temple and

"DON'T FIGHT AGAINST GOD"

preach the Gospel to all the people, and they did as they were instructed and caused quite a sensation.

Caiaphas thought they were still in prison, and he actually had the Sanhedrin brought together so that the Apostles could be formally charged. The idea was to end this thing once and for all. The Leader had been crucified, but His disciples were carrying on His work. Where would it end? So Caiaphas determined to destroy the leaders. He did not seem to realize that he would have to keep on dealing with a new lot of leaders, for this movement is spreading far and wide.

The Temple troops were dispatched to the prison, and they ordered the keepers standing on duty to open the doors and to bring out the prisoners. The officers actually watched as the doors were unlocked, and then heard the amazed cries of the sentries. Although the doors were all properly secured, the prison rooms were all empty. All those prisoners had escaped—who could say where they would be by now! Probably half-way to Beer Sheba, or maybe they had gone north to Galilee.

The officers reported back to the High Priest and the other leaders, and they could hardly believe their ears.

"Where will it all end?" was the question on every one's lips. "We've got to stop this nonsense somehow—it's getting out of hand!"

Suddenly a man came running up, out of breath, and he exclaimed, "You know those men you arrested and put in prison?"

"Yes, of course we do," one of the group answered. "Speak up man—what about them?"

"Well, they're all over there at the Temple, and they're publicly teaching, with a crowd of people listening!"

"Go and arrest them," Caiaphas instructed the captain of the troops, and they set off to do as they were ordered. They were careful not to act violently, for the amazing release from prison was known to the people and many believed this thing was of God.

"Come with us, please," they instructed Peter and John, as the leaders of the group.

John and the others looked to Peter, as though waiting for his decision.

"Obey those who have the rule over you," counselled the big fisherman. "Our Lord allowed Himself to be arrested and even bound. Let us also go before those same men who condemned Him to death."

The others quietly agreed, and without

"DON'T FIGHT AGAINST GOD"

any force or violence they set off with the captain and his troops, back to where Caiaphas was waiting, furious at the way he was being humiliated.

The captain himself was very relieved at how easy his task had proved. He knew full well that the people might have stoned him and his troops if he had attempted to arrest these men against their will.

Now the Apostles were arraigned as a group before the assembled Sanhedrin, and Caiaphas almost bellowed, so furious was he.

"Did we not clearly order you not to teach in this name of Jesus? Look what you've been doing! All Jerusalem is talking about you and your blasphemies! What are you trying to do — to have all of us blamed for the blood of that man whom we found guilty of blasphemy against God?"

Peter was the spokesman, but as he lifted up his voice, the others nodded their heads from time to time. It was clear they all agreed with everything he said.

"When it comes to a choice, we must obey God rather than men," Peter began. "Our God is the same God Whom our fathers served, and God has shown Himself in our midst. You yourselves were guilty of murder, and not just the murder of an ordinary Man. The One you killed was the Son of God, and God raised Him from the dead, to be a Prince and a Savior. Only through Him can there be forgiveness of sins, for Israel must repent and return to God through that Man Whom you crucified."

"Who do you think you are?" mocked Caiaphas. "You stand here as our prisoners, and you dare to call us murderers?"

Peter looked Caiaphas squarely in the face.

"We may be your prisoners, just as Jesus the Christ was your prisoner. But you could not keep Him sealed in a tomb, and you could not keep us locked in prison. How do you account for our release?"

For a moment there was intense silence, for Peter's statement was hard to answer. Then he continued. "We are God's special witnesses, and the Holy Spirit of God is working through us," he boldly declared. "The Holy Spirit works through us, His servants, because we are ready to obey Him!"

It seemed that pandemonium would break loose, for those words infuriated both Caiaphas and the other leaders as well. They were cut to the heart, and it was clear

"DON'T FIGHT AGAINST GOD"

from their shouting to each other that they were about to reach yet another illegal and unprincipled decision to bring in the death penalty, not on one innocent Man Who claimed to be the Son of God, but now on a whole group of men who claimed to be the special servants of the Holy Spirit of God Himself.

But suddenly a hush fell, and there was a strange silence. A gray-headed man had risen to his feet and had beckoned that he wished to be heard. It was, of course, Rabbi Gamaliel.

Gamaliel was a highly respected Pharisee, recognized as a great man among the members of the Sanhedrin. He was a doctor of the law, and all the people held him in very high esteem. When he stood to his feet, there was respectful silence. He called to the attendant to put the prisoners out of the room while he addressed the assembled members of the Council, and when that was done he said something like this:

"My brethren, we must be very careful in this matter. We should be careful because we are not sure what we are doing. There have been others who have risen and claimed to be great ones, such as Theudas—you will remember how about four hundred men joined themselves to him when he wanted to lead a movement against Rome. However, Theudas himself was slain, and those who obeyed him were scattered. His movement soon came to nothing. Then there was also that man Judas of Galilee who objected to the Roman system of taxing and a lot of people followed him. However, he also perished in the effort, and once again those who followed him were scattered far and wide.

"Now brethren, what I say is this. We should refrain from these men and leave them alone. If this thing they are talking about, if this new teaching and these works associated with it are of men, it will all come to nothing—just as with Theudas and with Judas. On the other hand it might just be something proceeding from God. If it is of God you cannot overthrow it—after all, if it is of God and you are attempting to overthrow it, you will find yourself in the foolish position of attempting to fight against God."

As I have said, Gamaliel was very highly respected by the members of the Council, and they listened to him respectfully. They talked about what he had said for a little while, but they agreed that it was the best thing to do.

"DON'T FIGHT AGAINST GOD"

So the attendants were told to bring the prisoners in again, and right then they were given a beating. They had not been found guilty of any offense, and indeed no charge could be properly laid against them, but there was the hope that they would recognize that it was dangerous to oppose Jewish traditions, and desist from their activities.

Caiaphas commanded them that they should never again speak in the name of Jesus, and then the Council allowed the prisoners to go free.

However, instead of the Apostles being afraid of Caiaphas and the High Priestly party, they actually rejoiced. They came back to the other disciples and told them what had happened, and literally they rejoiced that they had been counted worthy to suffer shame for the Lord Jesus Christ. Some of them were deeply aware of the fact that they had denied Him at the time of His greatest need as a Man, and now in a sense they were making amends.

Nor did they obey the commandment of the High Priest in this matter. They did not regard him as having authority to order them to cease from proclaiming Jesus. To them that would have meant obeying a man rather than obeying God. They even kept up their activities in the Temple, and also they preached from house to house, declaring that Jesus was the Christ.

In the days that have followed I have become increasingly amazed at the blindness of my own former colleagues. Our Scriptures clearly stated that a Messiah would come, born in Bethlehem, being a great Light in Galilee, giving hearing to the deaf and healing others, that He would die by crucifixion and would be buried with the rich, then would be raised from the dead. All this had been fulfilled before our eyes as it were. The evidences were there, with men and women all over Jerusalem, and indeed all over Galilee and Judea, able to testify to the amazing works that Jesus had undertaken on their persons. As I say, it is amazing. We expected a Messiah, but when One with Messianic claims appeared in our midst, we did not even investigate His claims seriously.

Jesus had denounced hypocrisy, and that hurt many, such as the priestly members of the Pharisee party. However they were indeed hypocrites, on a pretense making long prayers and doing their deeds so that they would have the praise of men. Jesus came and offered a new, vital, spiritual relationship with His heavenly Father, and they rejected His message. In rejecting His message they rejected His Person. Spritually, their eyes were indeed blind and their ears were deaf.

I am convinced that the years ahead will indeed show that these men were fighting against God, just as Gamaliel urged at that time when some of the followers of Jesus stood before the Council and boldly proclaimed that Jesus was the true Messiah of God.

Letter No. 14

Nicodemus Debates With The Rabbis

Now Lazarus, Nicodemus, and I walk carefully. We saw the ultimate of hatred as our brethren demanded the crucifixion of Jesus, and we know that their threats against us are not idle boasts. We have been careful not to be found alone, and we have avoided all those places where the chief priests and the scribes habitually gather.

Our crime? It is actually a shared "crime," in each case involving life and death. Nicodemus has not been hesitant to tell of his previously secret interview with Jesus, when Jesus taught him about new life, and made it clear (in retrospect) that He Himself must be "lifted up" in death before that new life could be known. As I have already said, while he stood next to me at the Cross Nicodemus suddenly saw spiritual realities clearly, as though scales had fallen from his eyes. He will never be the same again.

This presents a real problem for my colleagues, as Nicodemus has long been regarded as THE teacher in Israel. He has a wonderful ability to make profound teachings seem simple, and of course he has a great knowledge of our Scriptures. He now recognizes that many Scriptures have their fulfillment in Jesus, and he is not slow to say so. He has fearlessly declared his belief that the prophet Micah was speaking of Jesus when he declared that Bethlehem would be Messiah's birthplace, that Isaiah was pointing to Jesus when he wrote about Galilee seeing a great light, that our great King David was prophetically announcing that Jesus would die by crucifixion when he wrote in the Psalms, "They pierced my hands and my feet," and that David was also foretelling the resurrection and ascension of Jesus in that same Psalm when he exultantly exclaimed, "In the midst of my brethren I will sing the praises of God."

The fact is, in his own way Nicodemus has become an evangelist, a proclaimer of the Gospel, a preacher of the good news that eternal life is available because Christ died and rose again.

In these declarations he has not hesitated to claim that our own people were guilty of false judgment at various points, and he has even indicated some ways in which the rulers themselves unknowingly fulfilled prophecies within our Scriptures. Some of those are the ones to which I have referred, but there are many others.

Two such declarations by Nicodemus have been especially resented by the Chief Priests. One relates to John the Baptist, whom our people openly acknowledge was a prophet sent from God. They were not involved in the criminal illegality of his death: they rightly blame that on Herod Antipas who foolishly agreed to the whim of his mistress to have John beheaded. They denounced Antipas for that at the time, and they still do so.

They had not agreed with John's message, for his claim to be "The voice crying in the wilderness" was actually a direct challenge to the teachings of the Qumran community out by the Dead Sea, south of Jericho. They collectively claimed to be the fulfillment of that prophecy, and at first John appeared to accept that as authentic. He himself had joined the community for a time, full of pious objections to the way the Roman overlords exercised their authority over our people. However, he found himself out of sympathy with many of the practices of that monastic community, and he was not hesitant to let his personal views be known.

Then, as he continued to study our Scriptures, he came to a seemingly surprising conclusion. He remembered stories his mother had told him about his own birth. The angel of the Lord had appeared, and John grew up knowing he was a special child, one for whom the Lord had an unusual work.

His studies at Qumran and elsewhere led him to believe that the Lord's special work for him was to be the herald of the Messiah. So it was that he proclaimed that he, and not the Qumran community, was "the voice crying in the wilderness," and he went about urging men to prepare the way of the Lord and to make His paths straight. He was especially active in the Jericho area and the nearby villages.

Despite his opposition to the Teacher of Righteousness, as they called the leader of the Qumran community, many of our people listened to the teachings of this strange man lifting up his voice out by the

NICODEMUS DEBATES THE RABBIS

Jordan, and thousands flocked to be baptized by him.

All this is relevant to what I have said about Nicodemus, for he suddenly realized how illogical our former colleagues were. They acknowledged that John was a true prophet, and this meant that his major message must also be accepted as fact. That message was that he himself was merely a herald, a forerunner of One Whose coming he announced.

John had actually declared that Jesus was that One, and therefore, Nicodemus openly declared, if Jesus was a false Messiah, then John the Baptist also was a false prophet.

Our people gnashed their teeth. They had thought this whole movement would end when they destroyed its Founder, but that had not been the case. Now their own leading teacher was openly espousing the claims of the Nazarean, and was putting up logical arguments they could not explain away. It was all remarkably close to the spirit of Christ Himself. My colleagues hated Nicodemus for his forthrightness, especially because he too was accusing them of spritual blindness, just as Jesus had done.

Nicodemus readily acknowledged that

he himself had been blind, but now he saw clearly, and by his incisive interpretations he convinced many of his former colleagues that Jesus really was the Messiah.

"Take the Passover Lamb," he said one night to a group of serious young rabbis who had gathered to question him concerning his new-found faith. "God is not pleased with the sacrifice of a lamb for its own sake. It pointed on to a greater Sacrifice. Did not the Prophet Isaiah write about the Servant of the Lord, 'He is led as a lamb to the slaughter'? Jesus was that Suffering Servant, and John the Baptist understood something of that truth when he pointed to Jesus and declared, 'Behold—the Lamb of God Who takes away the sin of the world'."

One of those young Rabbis was a visitor to Jerusalem. He came from Tarsus, and it is said that he is destined for great things. He obviously had a good mind, but right from the first I have feared he can do us great damage. On this matter of the Lamb of God, he was quite forthright.

"You seem to think those animal sacrifices were saying the Anointed One would be a sacrifice to God. Is that what you are saying?"

"That is what I am saying," Nicodemus

NICODEMUS DEBATES THE RABBIS

agreed.

"Then surely you forgot that the Anointed One will be God's messenger, coming from the presence of God," he said coldly. "God's servant cannot be taken and killed like an animal."

Nicodemus was not to be silenced.

"At what time of the day is the Passover Lamb sacrificed?" he asked the young skeptic.

"At the time of the evening sacrifice—the 9th hour. You know that," the young man replied impatiently. (His name was Saul.)

"Yes," Nicodemus answered quietly. "I *do* know that. And that was the very time when I saw Jesus die on the cross. At the ninth hour He dismissed His own spirit."

Saul of Tarsus smiled patronizingly. "That's just a coincidence. He had to die some time and it has no special meaning that he died at the ninth hour."

"No Saul, you are wrong," Nicodemus insisted. "Our leaders decided he would not be destroyed on the feast day, yet that was the very day He DID die, and not only on the right day, but at the right minute. You may not know it, but the veil in the Temple was torn from the top to the bottom at that time—just when the High Priest was occupied with the sacrificial activities."

Saul got up to go. "You see signs and wonders everywhere," he declared. "There are many coincidences in life and I refuse to believe these things you are saying. You are too gullible Rabbi Nicodemus, too ready to believe anything about your Jesus." He moved toward the door, but paused to listen as Nicodemus declared, "You are blocking your spiritual ears Saul. You are kicking against the pricks. But Saul, we shall pray for you."

"Pray for yourself," Saul snarled. "You might need it." As he went, we knew he meant us harm.

Letter No. 15

Saul's Misguided Fury

Saul of Tarsus was a remarkable man. He himself was a Pharisee, born into a Pharisee family, and in fact he was a Roman citizen as well. By trade he was a leather worker, and actually had very good business contacts. He was of the tribe of Benjamin, and was highly respected by the members of the Sanhedrin. It was at times said that in coming days he would be a leading teacher in Israel. Rabbi Gamaliel spoke highly of him, and of course Gamaliel's estimate is taken seriously.

You know of the great sorrow we all experienced when that young man Stephen was stoned to death because he boldly declared that Jesus was the Just One of God, the One Who had been promised. He insisted that Jesus was the great Prophet to Whom Moses had pointed, and he also told the Jewish leaders that they were stiffnecked people, resisting the Holy Ghost as their fathers had done before them. He went so far as to tell them that just as their fathers had persecuted the prophets, so they now had betrayed and murdered the Just One of God. The leaders had refused to listen to the testimony of Stephen, and they cast him out of the city and then stoned him.

As they did that terrible deed, they actually laid their clothes down at the feet of a young man who kept charge of them. That young man was Saul of Tarsus. The accusations against Stephen were false, even as those against Jesus had been previously. However, in his misguided zeal Saul of Tarsus thought that it was the right thing to stone Stephen, this man who would be the first martyr for the cause of Jesus Christ.

Not satisfied with one man being killed in the cause of Jesus Christ, Saul of Tarsus set out on a totally misguided campaign of hate against all His followers. He consented to the death of Stephen, and thereby took part in an illegal and violent murder. Saul had much to do with the great persecution that took place against those who announced themselves as continuing disciples of Jesus. He entered into house after house, and if he found people were prepared to acknowledge that they were followers of Jesus he had men and women alike committed to prison in great numbers. As a result the disciples were scattered, but wherever they went they preached that Jesus was the Christ. Because of the persecution by Saul and others who were prepared to follow the dictates of the High Priest, the church was established, strengthened, and expanded.

As far as Saul was concerned, his guilt was great, and yet I have no doubt that this zealous man was quite misguided. He believed he was doing God a service by persecuting any who accepted Jesus as the Messiah.

He even went to the High Priest and asked for letters from him so that he could go to Damascus and search out any who dared to proclaim themselves as followers of Jesus as the Christ. He got the letters he asked for, and he was on his way to Damascus, with authority to have the people bound and brought back to Jerusalem if they would not renounce Jesus as the Christ.

On the way to Damascus he had a remarkable experience, for at midday he saw a great Light, greater than the sun,

and Jesus revealed Himself from heaven
to this man who apparently is especially
chosen of God to be a great witness to
the truths centering around Jesus the Messiah. The details have been told by others
and I will not repeat them at this point,
but that young man of such great promise
was converted to Jesus Christ at that
time. Now he goes boldly into the synagogues, reasoning with Jews and explaining to them that our own Scriptures clearly
pointed to Jesus as the Messiah.

As a result, the High Priestly party
determined to kill Saul also. One wonders
where it will end. Will they continue on
their campaign of murder, hatred, and evil
indefinitely? Will they never understand
that they are spiritually deaf and blind?
What *will* it take to convince them?

The death sentence has been pronounced against Saul. That same death
sentence has been pronounced against
Lazarus whom Jesus raised from the dead,
and it has also been pronounced against
many others who dare to insist that Jesus
is indeed the Christ, the very Son of God.
I myself go in fear of my life, not knowing
when I shall be apprehended, imprisoned,
beaten, and perhaps even forfeit my own
life. Saul knows that he goes in danger of

his life, but he seems to have no fear of those who were once his friends and his confidantes. He has told others that he regards himself as the chief of sinners, because of the way he persecuted the followers of Jesus. He also believes that the grace of God has been shown to him in a special way, because the world is to know that Jesus is able to save to the uttermost all those who will come to God by Him. Jesus the Christ lives to make intercession, and His cry on the cross was, "Father forgive them, for they know not what they do." Saul is one who has been forgiven, because he has recognized that Christ died for him. On that cross at the place called Golgotha, the Place of the Skull, Jesus died for Saul of Tarsus, and for Joseph of Arimathea. We live, because Christ died. We face death daily because Christ lives. We rejoice in the hope of Christ's return when His Church has finished her appointed time on earth. We serve the risen, living Christ. He walks with us. What more can we ask?

Letter No. 16

I Must Go Into Hiding . . . .

This will be the last letter I shall write for a while, as it is becoming increasingly clear that I must go into hiding. In fact, I shall necessarily be brief, for it would not surprise me to hear my door being broken down at any moment as soldiers come to arrest me. However, it may be some time yet, for here at Arimathea we are some distance from our beloved Jerusalem, and the spreading hatred is not yet intense here. Nevertheless, we have heard of arrests not far from us, and the disciples have urged me to withdraw for some time.

Remarkable things have taken place in these weeks. I have already written that the young man Saul of Tarsus has been converted, and that he has been debating with some members of the priestly party, convincing many that He Whom we worship is in fact our promised Messiah.

Probably God has some special work for this energetic and highly intelligent young man, with his vast knowledge of the Scriptures of our people.

Another young man who impresses me is himself a Gentile. He is actually a medical doctor, but he has a special interest in history. He has been collecting material relating to the life and teachings of Jesus. He impresses me as being a very thorough young man, and he has talked to many of those who had close contact with Jesus in the three and a half years of His public ministry.

In my own case, he was especially interested to hear firsthand of my experience with Pilate. He also asked me at length about the actual burying of the Body of Jesus in my tomb. What a wonderful privilege that was: I keep marveling at the grace of God in allowing such a privilege to me, a mere failing mortal. In our priestly Manual, known as Leviticus, we learn that even the ashes of the sin offering had to be poured out into a clean place. Now I realize that Jesus Himself was our Sin Offering, and when His Body was placed in my new tomb, that was the "clean place"! God gave me the great privilege of providing that place so that the type could be fulfilled, and I thank Him for His grace.

As I say, Luke has been asking me about these things. I think it is fitting that such a man should do his best to ensure that a proper record is kept of the life of Jesus, and I am sure it will be accepted widely by those who believe that Jesus is indeed the Christ, the Son of God.

I shall hide this manuscript in a good place. I did think of the very cave where Lazarus had been buried, but I shall keep my options open. It will be in a safe place, and possibly some of these things I have said will be of value to men in a coming day.

I personally have no regrets that I am about to leave my lovely home and the comforts to which I have grown accustomed. It was my privilege to allow Jesus the Christ to rest in my tomb, and it was my joy to know that He had risen from the dead and left that tomb behind Him. Now it is my privilege to go forth to Him, outside the camp as it were, bearing His reproach. What I should like to do is to write a letter for the church showing that Jesus is the fulfillment of the Old Testament prophecies—of the types. I should like to show that He is greater than all men, greater than angels, greater than the Temple, and greater than all the offerings and the sacrifices. He Himself is the fulfillment of all those types.

There is much more I should like to say. The Qumran Community taught there would be four heavenly Messiah-figures, for they could not understand how the prophecies could relate to only one Messiah.

As I said above, I should like to write at length and explain these things to my Hebrew brethren. So much could be written—so much needs to be explained. My people are blind, but when we understand that Jesus was and is the Messiah, it all becomes plain to see.

Jesus Himself was the Great Prophet like Moses. He is the Son of David, Israel's rightful King. He is also the Great High Priest of Aaron's order—for He is the Good Shepherd Who is also the Lamb: He was both Offerer and Offering. He fulfilled the types of those Aaronic sacrifices.

He is also the High Priest Who lives forever, the Great High Priest after the order of Melchizedec. That King's personal history was partly an illustration of Jesus, the eternal King Who lives forever. His sacrifice of Himself was made once for all,

I MUST GO INTO HIDING . . .

and now He has sat down at the right hand of God. His sacrificial work will never be repeated.

So those Qumran teachers and writers need not have looked for four Messiahs. All the prophecies come together in one Person alone, even in Jesus Who is the Messiah of Israel and the Savior of the World. He is also the Suffering Servant of Whom Isaiah wrote prophetically, the One led as a Lamb to the slaughter Who also sees the travail of His soul and is satisfied.

Someone must write these things for our Hebrew brethren, both in Judea and scattered far and wide. Perhaps I shall make that a special activity while I am in hiding. Possibly I shall do it in association with others of my Jewish brethren. How, I am not sure, but I am convinced that it must be done.

If I am to write about these things myself, I shall of course be willing to do so, as the Lord directs. I am convinced that someone surely must put these things down clearly in a letter to the Hebrews . . . . As I say, perhaps several of us should be associated in such an important work. Time will tell. If I do so myself I think I shall do it anonymously, for otherwise my time on earth would certainly be ended by my former colleagues.

But I must go, for my friends have arrived and preparations have been completed to take me to safety. I go in secrecy at the moment, but I go in the presence of Him Who was raised from the dead and has promised to be with those who serve Him—unto the end of the age.

I go forth, looking unto Jesus the Author and the Finisher of my faith. That faith was especially confirmed when Jesus the Christ left my tomb behind Him. He showed Himself alive by so many proofs for forty days, and then He ascended to the right hand of His Father on high. Praise God for the victory of His resurrection and for the blessed assurance of eternity in His presence.